RESIDENT EVIL™

UNDERWORLD

DATE DUE		
NOV 0 9 2012	JAN 0 3 2013	
SEP 2 8 2013		

ALSO BY S.D. PERRY
AND AVAILABLE FROM TITAN BOOKS

RESIDENT EVIL™

RESIDENT EVIL™

UNDERWORLD

S.D. PERRY

TITAN BOOKS

RESIDENT EVIL: UNDERWORLD
Print edition ISBN: 9781781161807
E-book edition ISBN: 9781781161890

Published by Titan Books
A division of Titan Publishing Group Ltd
144 Southwark Street, London SE1 0UP

First edition October 2012
1 3 5 7 9 10 8 6 4 2

A CIP catalogue record for this title is available
from the British Library.

Printed and bound in the United States.

Did you enjoy this book? We love to hear from our readers.
Please email us at readerfeedback@titanemail.com or write to
us at Reader Feedback at the above address.

To receive advance information, news, competitions, and
exclusive offers online, please sign up for the Titan newsletter
on our website: **www.titanbooks.com**

FOR MY EDITOR, MARCO PALMIERI

"There are a thousand hacking at the branches of evil to one who is striking at the root."

HENRY DAVID THOREAU

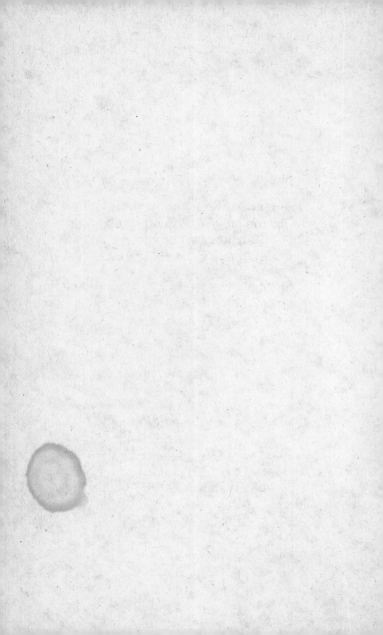

PROLOGUE

Associated Press, October 6, 1998

THOUSANDS KILLED AS FIRE SWEEPS THROUGH MOUNTAIN COMMUNITY, MYSTERIOUS ILLNESS MAY BE INVOLVED

NEW YORK, NY—The secluded mountain community of Raccoon City, PA, has officially been declared a disaster area by state and federal officials, as dedicated firefighters continue to wage war against the dying blazes and the death toll continues to rise. It is now estimated that over seven thousand people were killed by the explosive fires that raged through Raccoon in the early hours of Sunday, October 4. It is being called the worst U.S. disaster in terms of lives lost since the industrial age, and as national aid organizations and international press flock to the blockades surrounding the still burning ruins of the city, shocked friends and family of Raccoon citizens have been gathering, waiting for word in nearby Latham.

National Disaster Control (NDC) Director Terrence Chavez, coordinator for the combined efforts of the multiple firefighting and emergency teams, released a statement to the press last night stating that barring unforeseen complications, he expects the last of the flames to be extinguished before midweek—but that it may be months before the origin of the fire is determined, as well as whether or not arson was involved. Said Chavez, "The magnitude of the damage in terms of area alone is going to make finding the answers a great undertaking, but the answers are there. We will get to the bottom of this, whatever it takes."

As of 6 A.M. today, seventy-eight survivors have been found, and their names and conditions withheld; they have been transported to an undisclosed federal facility for observation and/or treatment. Initial reports by HazMat teams suggest that an unknown illness may be responsible for the incredible number of victims, as infected citizens were unable to escape due to the possibly incapacitating sickness. There is the further suggestion that the disease may have induced violent psychosis in some of those infected. Members of private and federal disease-control centers have called for extending the quarantine boundaries, and although no official statement has been released, there have been several "leaked" descriptions of physical and biological abnormalities in many of the victims. Said one source, a worker for a federal assessment team, "Some of those people weren't just burned or dead from smoke inhalation. I saw people who'd been killed by gunshot wounds or stabbings, [and] other forms of violence. I saw people who'd obviously been sick, dead, or dying long before the fire ever hit. The fire was bad—terrible—but it's not the only disaster that occurred there, I'd bet money on it."

Raccoon City was in the news earlier this year when a series of unusual murders rocked the community. These were apparently unmotivated slayings, of extreme violence, and several involved cannibalism; already, tentative connections are being made by local press near Raccoon between the eleven unsolved murders from last summer and the rumors of mass violence prior to the consuming flames.

Mr. Chavez refused to confirm or deny the rumors, saying only that investigations into the tragedy will be thorough...

Nationwide Today, A.M. Edition, October 10, 1998
RACCOON DEATH TOLL RISES AS SEARCH AND RESCUE TEAMS COMBINE EFFORTS

NEW YORK, NY—The official body count now stands at just under 4500, with the blackened ruins of Raccoon City still being combed for additional victims of the apocalypse that took place early last Sunday morning. As a nation's mourning begins, over six hundred men and women are working to uncover the reasons behind the destruction of the once peaceful community. Local relief organizations, scientists, soldiers, federal agents, and corporate research teams have come together in a show of determination and purpose, pooling resources and accepting delegated responsibilities in order to get to the truth.

NDC Director Terrence Chavez, the official head of the effort, has been joined by top researchers from disease-control centers all around the world, national security agents from several federal branches, and a privately funded team of microbiologists from Umbrella, Inc., the pharmaceutical company, which is investigating the possibility that there may be a connection between their chemical lab on the outskirts of the city and the strange infection now being called "Raccoon syndrome."

Initial studies of this illness have been vague and inconclusive, says Umbrella team leader Dr. Ellis Benjamin, "but we're convinced that the citizens of Raccoon were infected with *something*, either accidentally or intentionally. All we know at this point is that it doesn't seem to have been airborne, and that the final result was rapid cellular disintegration and death; we still don't know if it was bacterial or viral, or what the symptoms were, but we won't rest until we've exhausted all of our resources. Whatever the findings, and whether or not Umbrella materials were a part of it, we're committed to seeing this through to the end. It's the least we can do, considering how much our company owes the people of Raccoon." The

Umbrella chemical plant and administration facilities in Raccoon City provided nearly a thousand local jobs.

The 142 survivors are still being held in quarantine for observation and questioning at an undisclosed location. While their identities are still being protected, the FBI has released a statement listing medical conditions. Seventeen survivors suffered minor injuries but are in stable condition, seventy-nine are still on a critical list following surgical procedures, and forty-six of the survivors, while not injured, have suffered some major mental or emotional breakdown. There is no confirmation as to whether or not any are infected with the syndrome, but the statement did include a reference to survivor's stories that verified the existence of the infection.

Gen. Martin Goldmann, overseer of military operations in the ravaged city, is hopeful that all of those still missing will be found within the next seven days. "We've already got four hundred people out there working twenty-four/seven, searching for survivors and running identification checks—and I just got word that another two hundred will be coming in on Monday..."

Fort Worth Bugler, October 18, 1998

POSSIBLE CONSPIRACY BY CITY EMPLOYEES IN RACCOON TRAGEDY

FORT WORTH, TX—New evidence uncovered by cleanup crews in Raccoon City, PA, indicates that the "Raccoon syndrome," the disease responsible for the majority of the 7200 deaths that have occurred in Raccoon as of this writing, may have been unleashed upon the unsuspecting populace by Raccoon Police Chief Brian Irons and several members of the Special Tactics and Rescue Service (S.T.A.R.S.).

At a press conference, held early yesterday evening by FBI spokesman Patrick Weeks, NDC Director Terrence Chavez, and Dr. Robert Heiner—called in by Umbrella team leader Dr. Ellis Benjamin—Weeks revealed that there is strong circumstantial evidence that the disaster in Raccoon was the result of a terrorist act that went horribly wrong. The subsequent fires that have nearly wiped out the small city may have been an attempt by Irons or one of his accomplices to cover up the disastrous effects of the spill.

According to Weeks, several documents were found in the wreckage of the RPD building that implicate Irons as the ringleader of a conspiracy to take hostage the Umbrella chemical plant on the outskirts of the city. Allegedly, Irons was furious with city officials over the suspension of the S.T.A.R.S. in late July for their mishandling of a multiple murder investigation—the now well-documented cannibal slayings that took the lives of eleven people early last summer. The Raccoon S.T.A.R.S. were suspended after a helicopter crash in the last week of July that claimed the lives of six team members. The five surviving S.T.A.R.S. members were suspended without pay after evidence suggested drug or alcohol abuse in connection to the crash— and while Irons publicly advocated the suspension of his elite squad, the documents found indicate that Irons meant to threaten Mayor Devlin Harris and several City Council members with a spill of extremely volatile and dangerous chemicals unless certain financial demands were met. Weeks went on to say that Irons had a history of emotional instability, and that the documents—correspondence between Irons and an accomplice—revealed a plan by Irons to extort ransom from Raccoon and then flee the country. The accomplice is named only as "C.R.," but there are also references to "J.V.," "B.B," and "R.C."—all initials for four of the five suspended S.T.A.R.S.

Said Terrence Chavez, "Assuming these documents are accurate, Irons and his crew had planned to storm the Umbrella plant at the end of September, which would correspond exactly to the timeline described by Dr. Heiner for the Raccoon syndrome to achieve full amplification. We're currently operating under the assumption that the takeover did take place, and that an unexpected accident occurred with cataclysmic results. At this time, we don't know if Mr. Irons or any of the S.T.A.R.S. are still alive, but they are wanted for questioning. We've released a national APB and all of our international airports and border patrols have been alerted. We urge anyone with information relating to this case to come forward."

Dr. Heiner, a renowned microbiologist as well as an associate member of Umbrella's Biohazardous Materials Division, stated that the exact mix of chemicals released in Raccoon may never be known. "It's obvious that Irons and his people didn't know what they were handling—and with Umbrella continuously developing new variations of enzyme syntheses, bacterial growth mediums, and viral repressors, the lethal compound was almost certainly an accidental aggregation. With the possible combinations of materials numbering in the millions, the odds of duplicating the Raccoon syndrome mix are astronomical."

The S.T.A.R.S. national director wasn't available for comment, but Lida Willis, regional spokesperson for the organization, has gone on record as saying that they "are shocked and saddened" by the disaster, and would devote every available agent to the search for the missing S.T.A.R.S. team members, as well as for any contacts they might still have within the network.

Ironically, the documents were found by one of Umbrella's search teams...

ONE

"Go, GO, GO!" David shouted, and John Andrews hit the gas, whipping the minivan around a tight corner as gunfire thundered through the cold Maine night.

John had spotted the two unmarked black sedans only a moment before, which had barely given the team enough time to arm themselves. Whoever was on their ass—Umbrella or the S.T.A.R.S. or the local cops—it didn't matter, it was all Umbrella—

"Get us lost, John!" David called, somehow managing to sound cool and controlled even as bullets riddled the back of the van. It was the accent—*he always sounds like that, and where the hell's Falworth?*

John felt scattered, his thoughts racing and jumbled; he kicked ass on a mission, but sneak attacks bit the bone—

—right on Falworth and head for the strip—Christ, ten more minutes and we would've been gone—

It had been too long since John had been in combat, and never in the midst of a car chase. He was good, but it was a *minivan*—

Bam bam bam!

Someone in the back of the van was returning fire, shooting out of the open back window. The nine-millimeter explosions in the tight space were as loud as the voice of an irate God, pounding at John's ears and making it even harder to focus.

Ten more goddamn minutes.

Ten minutes from the airstrip, where the chartered flight would be waiting. It was like a bad joke—weeks of hiding, waiting, not taking any risks, and then getting tagged on the way out of the damn *country*.

John hung on to the wheel as they shot down 6th Street, the van too heavy to outmaneuver the sedans. Even without five people and a shitload of artillery, the bulky, boxy knockoff mini wasn't exactly a power-house. David had bought it because it was so nondescript, so unlikely to be noticed, and they were paying for it—if they managed to shake their pursuers, it'd be a small miracle. Their only chance was to try to find traffic, play some dodge. It was dangerous, but so was getting run off the road and shot to death.

"Clip!" Leon shouted, and John shot a look in the rearview, saw that the young cop was crouched at the back window next to David. They'd taken out the back seats for the trip to the airstrip, all the more room for weapons—but that also meant no seatbelts; take a corner too fast and bodies would be flying—

Bam! Bam! Two more blasts from the sedan assholes, maybe from a .38. John gave the shuddering van a little more pedal as Leon returned fire with a Browning nine-millimeter. Leon Kennedy was their best shot, David probably had him trying to draw bead on the tires—

—*best shot next to me, anyway, and how the hell am I going to get us lost in Exeter, Maine, at eleven o'clock on a weeknight? There is no traffic*—

One of the women tossed Leon a mag, John didn't have time to see which one as he jerked the wheel right, heading for downtown. With a smoking squeal of rubber on asphalt, the mini teetered around the corner of Falworth, heading east. The airstrip was west, but John didn't figure that anyone in the van was worrying much about getting to the plane on time.

First things first, gotta ditch Umbrella's hired goons. Doubt there's room on the charter for all of us—

John saw red and blue light in the mirror, saw that at least one of the sedans had put a flasher on the roof. Maybe they *were* cops, which would really suck. Umbrella's job of spin control had been thorough—thanks to them, every cop in the country probably believed that their small team was at least partly responsible for what had happened to Raccoon. The S.T.A.R.S. were being played, too—some of the higher-ups had sold out, but the agents in the trenches probably had no idea that their organization had become a puppet of the pharmaceutical company—

—*which makes it a hell of a lot harder to shoot back.*

No one on their makeshift team wanted innocents to get hurt; being misled by Umbrella wasn't a crime, and if the sedan teams were cops—

"No antennae, no warning, not cops!" Leon called, and John had time to feel about a second's worth of relief before he saw the barricades looming in front of them, the roadwork sign propped next to the blocked street. He saw the white circle of a man's face above an orange vest, the man holding a sign that said "Slow," the man dropping the sign and diving for cover—

—and it would've been funny except they were doing eighty and had maybe three seconds before they hit.

* * *

"Hang on!" John screamed, and Claire pushed her legs against the van wall, saw David grab hold of Rebecca, Leon snatching at the handle—

—and the van was screeching, jerking, and bucking like a wild horse, spinning sideways—

—and Claire actually *felt* open space beneath the right side of the van as her body was compressed to the left, the back of her neck crunching painfully against the tire well.

—*oh hell*—

David shouted something but Claire didn't hear it over the squealing brakes, didn't understand until David dove to the right, Rebecca scrambling right next to him—

—and *wham,* the van dropped back to the ground with a terrific bounce and John seemed to have it under control again—but there was still the piercing screech of locked brakes coming from—

CRASH!

The explosion of metal and shattering glass behind them was so close that Claire's heart skipped a beat. She turned, looked out the back with the others and saw that one of the cars had barreled into a roadwork barricade—a barricade they'd probably come within a second or two of bashing into themselves. She caught just a glimpse of a crumpled hood, of broken windows and a stream of oily smoke, and then the second sedan was blocking her view, shrieking around the corner and continuing the chase.

"Sorry 'bout that," John called back to them, sounding anything but; he seemed wired with adrenaline-pumped glee.

In the few weeks since she and Leon had joined up with the fugitive ex-S.T.A.R.S., she'd discovered that John would make jokes about anything. It was simultaneously his most endearing and most annoying trait.

"Everyone alright?" David asked, and Claire nodded, saw Rebecca do the same.

"Took a whack but I'm okay," Leon said, rubbing his arm with a pained expression. "But I don't think—"

BAM!

Whatever Leon didn't think was cut off by the powerful blast that slammed into the back of the van.

Still most of a block away, the sedan's passenger had fired a shotgun at them; a few inches higher and the pellets would have come in through the window.

"John, change of plans," David called as the van swerved, his cool, authoritative voice rising over the noise of the screaming engines. "We're in their sights—"

Before he could finish, John took a hard left. Rebecca fell backwards, nearly crashing into Claire. The van was now headed down a quiet suburban street.

"Hold on to your butts," John called over his shoulder.

Chill night air whipped through the van, dark houses flying by as John picked up speed. Leon and David were already reloading, crouched behind the metal half-door. Claire exchanged a look with Rebecca, who looked as unhappy about their situation as she felt. Rebecca Chambers was ex-S.T.A.R.S., she'd worked with Claire's brother, Chris, as well as undertaking a recent Umbrella operation with David and John, also ex-S.T.A.R.S.—but the young woman had been trained as a medic with a background in biochemistry. Marksmanship wasn't her forte—even Claire was a better shot—and she was the only person in the van who hadn't had any real training...

...*unless you count surviving Raccoon.*

Claire shuddered involuntarily as John took a hard right, veering wide around a parked truck, the sedan gaining ground. Raccoon City; the scratches and bruises on Claire's body hadn't even faded yet, and she knew that Leon's shoulder was still giving him pain—

BAM!

Another shotgun blast from behind, but it went wide and high.

This time...

"Change of plans," David said, his crisp British accent calming, like the voice of reason and logic in the midst of chaos. It was no wonder he'd been a S.T.A.R.S. captain.

"Everyone brace for an impact. John, just past your next turn, bring us to a stop. Hit and run, alright?"

David brought his knees up, wedging his feet against the van's wall. "They want us so badly, let them have us."

Claire slid over and pushed her feet against the back of the passenger seat, knees bent and head down. Rebecca moved closer to David, and Leon sidled back so that his head was close to Claire's. They locked gazes and Leon smiled faintly.

"This is *nothin'*," he said, and in spite of her fear, Claire found herself smiling back at him. After making it through the madness of Raccoon City, skirting the murderous Umbrella creatures and crazed humans—not to mention their extremely narrow escape from explosive death when Umbrella's secret facilities blew up—compared to all that, a simple car wreck was like a Sunday picnic.

Yeah, just keep telling yourself that, her mind

whispered, and then she didn't think anything at all, because the van was swerving around a corner and John was pumping the brakes and they were about to get hit by about a ton and a half of fast moving metal and glass.

* * *

David inhaled and exhaled deeply, relaxing his muscles as best he could, the squeal of brakes coming up fast from behind—

—and *wham*, violent motion, a sense of incredible vibration, a second that seemed to stretch for an endless and silent eternity—

—and the noise coming immediately after— breaking glass and the sound of a tin can being crushed amplified a million times. David was jerked forward and back, heard Rebecca emit a strangled gasp—

—and it was over, and John was already hitting the gas as David rolled to his knees, raising his Beretta. He shot a look out the back and saw that the sedan was motionless, skewed across the dark street, the front grill and headlamps smashed all to hell. The slumped, shadowy figures behind the spidered glass were as still as the ruined car.

Not that we fared much better...

The inexpensive green minivan he'd bought specifically for their ride to the airfield no longer had a bumper, tail lights, a rear license plate—or, he imagined, any possible method for opening the back gate; the door was a warped and crunched-up mass of useless metal.

No great loss. David Trapp despised minivans, and it wasn't as though they'd planned on taking it to Europe. The important thing was that they were still alive—and that—for the moment at least—they'd managed to avoid the infinitely long arm of Umbrella's wrath.

As they sped away from the wrecked car, David turned and regarded the others, reflexively putting a hand out to help Rebecca up. Since the ill-fated mission to the Umbrella lab on the coast, he'd grown quite attached to the young woman, as had John. The rest of his team hadn't survived—

He shook off the thought before it could take hold, and called up to John that they should circle back toward their original destination, staying away from major streets. A bad break that they'd been spotted just as they were leaving—but not all that surprising, however. Umbrella had staked Exeter out two months earlier, right after they'd returned from Caliban Cove. It had only been a matter of time.

"Nice trick, David," Leon said. "I'll have to remember that next time I get chased by Umbrella goons."

David nodded uncomfortably. He liked Leon and Claire, but wasn't so sure how he felt about two more people looking to him for leadership. He could understand it with John and Rebecca, they'd at least been part of the S.T.A.R.S. before—but Leon was a rookie cop from Raccoon and Claire was a college student who just happened to be Chris Redfield's little sister. When he'd made the decision to break from the S.T.A.R.S. after finding out about their connection to Umbrella, he hadn't expected to continue leading, hadn't wanted to—

—*but it wasn't my decision to make, was it...* he hadn't asked for their allegiance, or offered himself up as decision maker—and it didn't matter, that was just the way things had turned out. In war, one didn't always have the luxury of choice.

David glanced around at the others before staring out the back, watching the homes and buildings slip past in the cold dark. Everyone seemed a bit subdued, always the aftermath of an adrenaline rush. Rebecca was unloading clips and repacking the weapons, Leon and Claire sitting close together across from her, not talking. Those two were usually joined at the hip, and were still as tight as they'd been since David, John, and Rebecca had picked them up just outside of Raccoon less than a month earlier, dirty and damaged and reeling from their run-in with Umbrella. David didn't think there was a romantic connection there, at least not yet; it was more likely their shared nightmare. Nearly dying together could be quite a bonding experience.

As far as David knew, Leon and Claire were the only survivors of the Raccoon disaster who knew about Umbrella's T-Virus spill. The child they'd had with them had only had the faintest idea, although

Claire had been very careful to shield the little girl from the truth. Sherry Birkin didn't need to know that her parents had been responsible for the creation of Umbrella's most powerful bioweapons; better that she remember her mother and father as decent people...

"David? Anything wrong?"

He shook himself out of his mental wanderings and nodded at Claire. "I'm sorry. Yes, I'm fine. Actually, I was thinking about Sherry; how is she?"

Claire smiled, and David was struck again by how she brightened when Sherry's name came up. "She's good, she's settling in. Kate is nothing like her sister, a definite plus. And Sherry likes her."

David nodded again. Sherry's aunt had seemed nice, but beyond that, she'd be able to protect Sherry if Umbrella decided to track the girl down; Kate Boyd was a fiercely competent criminal lawyer, one of the best in California. Umbrella would do well to stay away from the Birkins' only child.

Too bad the same doesn't apply to us; wouldn't that make things quite a lot easier...

Rebecca had finished reorganizing their rather impressive cache of weapons. She scooted over to sit next to him, brushing a loose strand of hair off her forehead. Her eyes much older than the rest of her face; barely nineteen, she'd already lived through two Umbrella incidents. Technically, she had more experience than any of them as far as the pharmaceutical company went.

Rebecca didn't speak for a moment, staring out at

the passing streets. When she finally spoke, she kept her voice low, her sharp gaze studying him intently.

"Do you think they're still alive?"

He wouldn't bother feeding her a sunny picture; young as she was, the girl had a knack for seeing through people.

"I don't know," he said, careful not to let the others overhear. Claire wanted desperately to reunite with her brother. "I doubt it. We should have heard from them. Either they're afraid of being traced, or..."

Rebecca sighed. Not surprised, but not happy. "Yeah. Even if they couldn't get through to us—Texas still has the scrambler up, don't they?"

David nodded. Texas, Oregon, Montana—all open channels with S.T.A.R.S. members who could still be trusted, and they hadn't gotten a call in over a month. The last message had been from Jill; David knew it by heart. In fact, it had been haunting him daily for weeks.

"Safe and sound in Austria. Barry and Chris tracking lead at UHQ, looks promising. Get ready."

Ready to join them, to call in the few waiting troops that he and John had managed to network. Ready to storm Umbrella's *real* headquarters, the power behind it all. Ready to strike against the evil at its source. Jill and Barry and Chris had gone to Europe to find out where the true leaders of Umbrella's hidden purpose were secreted, starting at international HQ in Austria—and had promptly disappeared.

"Heads up, kids," John called from the front, and

David looked away from Rebecca's unsmiling face, looked out to see they were already at the airfield.

Whatever had happened to their friends, they'd find out soon enough.

TWO

Rebecca strapped herself into the tiny seat of the tiny plane and looked out the window, wishing that David had chartered a jet. A giant, solid, can't-possibly-be-unsafe-'cause-it's-so-damned-big jet. From where she sat, she could see the propellers on the wing of the aircraft—*propellers*, like on a kid's toy.

Bet this puppy will sink like a rock, though, once it falls out of the sky at a few hundred miles an hour and slams into the ocean...

"Just so you know, this is the kind of plane that's always killing rock stars and the like. Just as they make it off the ground, a big gust of wind knocks them right back down."

Rebecca looked up to see John's grinning face; he was hanging over the seats in front of her, his massive arms folded across the headrests. He probably needed two seats to himself; John wasn't just big, he was body-builder huge, two hundred forty pounds of muscle packed into his six-foot-six frame.

"We'll be lucky to get off at all, dragging your fat ass up there," Rebecca shot back, and was rewarded with a flash of concern in John's dark eyes. He'd broken a couple of ribs and punctured a lung on his last mission, less than three months before, and still wasn't up to pumping iron. For as burly and macho as John was, she knew he was vain about his looks, and had absolutely *hated* not being able to work out.

John grinned wider, the deep brown of his skin crinkling. "Yeah, you're probably right; a few hundred feet off the ground and *wham*, that's all she wrote."

She never should have told him that this was only the second flight she'd ever been on (the first was when she accompanied David to Exeter for the mission to Caliban Cove). It was exactly the kind of thing on which John got off cracking jokes—

The plane started to rumble all around them, the engine whining up into a deep hum that made Rebecca grit her teeth. Damned if she was going to let John see how nervous she was; she looked back out the window and saw Leon and Claire walking toward the metal steps. Apparently, the weapons were all loaded up.

"Where's David?" Rebecca asked, and John shrugged.

"Talking to the pilot. We've only got the one, you know, some friend of a friend of some guy in Arkansas. Not many pilots willing to smuggle people into Europe, I guess..."

John leaned closer, dropping his voice to a fake

whisper, his grin fading. "I hear he drinks. We got him cheap 'cause he crashed some soccer team into the side of a mountain."

Rebecca laughed, shaking her head. "You win. I'm terrified, okay?"

"Okay. That's all I wanted," John said mildly, and turned around as Leon and Claire walked into the small cabin. They moved back to the middle of the plane, taking the two seats across the aisle from where Rebecca was sitting. David had mentioned that the area over the wings was the most stable, although it wasn't like there was that much of a choice—there were only twenty seats.

"Ever flown before?" Claire asked, leaning out into the aisle, looking a little nervous herself.

Rebecca shrugged. "Once. You?"

"Couple of times, but always on big airliners, DC 747s or -27s, I forget. I don't even know what this thing is."

"It's a DHC 8 Turbo," Leon said. "I think. David mentioned it at some point…"

"It's a killer, is what it is." John's deep voice floated over the seats. "A rock with wings."

"John, sweetie… shut up," Claire said amiably.

John cackled, obviously pleased to have somebody new to play with.

David appeared at the front of the cabin, stepping through the curtained area that led to the cockpit, and John broke off, their collective attention turning toward him.

"It seems that we're ready to go," David said. "Our pilot, Captain Evans, has assured me that all systems are fully functional and we'll be taking off in just a moment. He's asked that we remain seated until he's given us leave to do otherwise. Um—the restroom is just back of the cockpit, and there's a small refrigerator at the rear of the plane with sandwiches and drinks..."

His voice trailed off, and he looked as if there was something else he wanted to say but wasn't sure what it was. It was a look that Rebecca had seen often enough in the past few weeks, a kind of uneasy uncertainty. Since the day that Raccoon had been blown to shit, she supposed they'd all had that look at one time or another...

...because they shouldn't have been able to do it. That should have been the end, and it wasn't, and now we're all more freaked out than any of us wants to admit.

When news of the disaster first hit the papers, they had all been so certain that this time Umbrella wouldn't be able to cover its tracks. The spill at the Spencer estate had been small, easy enough to write off after fire gutted the mansion and surrounding buildings; the facility at Caliban Cove had been on private land and was too isolated for anyone to know about—again, Umbrella had swept up the broken pieces and kept it quiet.

Raccoon City, though. Thousands of people dead— and Umbrella had walked away from it smelling like a rose, after planting false evidence and getting their scientists to lie for them. It should have been impossible; it had disheartened them all. What chance did a handful of fugitives have against a multi-billion-dollar conglomerate that could kill an entire city and get away with it?

David had decided not to say anything at all. He nodded briskly and then walked back to join them, pausing next to Rebecca's seat.

"Do you need some company?"

She could see that he was trying to be supportive—and she could also see that he was tired. He'd been up late the night before, double-checking every detail of their trip.

"Nah, I'm okay," she said, smiling up at him, "and I've always got John to talk me through it."

"You know it, baby," John called loudly, and David nodded, giving her shoulder a light squeeze before moving to the seats behind her.

He needs the rest. We all do, and it's a long flight—so why do I have the feeling that we're not going to get any?

Nerves, that was all.

The engine sound got louder, higher, and with a stuttering jerk, the plane started to move forward. Rebecca clutched the arm rests on either side and closed her eyes, thinking that if she had the guts to go up against Umbrella, she could certainly survive a plane ride.

Even if she couldn't, it was too late to change her mind; they were on their way, no turning back.

* * *

They'd been in the air for only twenty minutes, and already Claire was nodding off, half-leaning against Leon's shoulder. Leon was tired, too, but knew he wasn't going to get to sleep so easily. He was hungry, for one thing—and then there was the fact that he still wasn't sure if he was doing the right thing.

Great time to think about it, now that you're pretty much committed, his mind whispered sarcastically. Maybe you could just ask them to drop you off in London or something, you could hang out in a pub until they're all finished... or dead.

Leon told himself to shut up, sighing a little. He was committed; what Umbrella had been doing wasn't just criminal, it was evil—or at least as close to evil as some money-grubbing corporate dickheads could get. They'd murdered thousands, created bioweapons capable of murdering *billions*, wiped out his carefully planned future and been responsible for the death of Ada Wong, a woman he'd respected and liked. They'd helped each other through some rough spots on that terrible night in Raccoon; without her, he never would have gotten out alive.

He believed in what David and his people were doing, and it wasn't that he was afraid, that wasn't it at all...

Leon sighed again. He'd given the matter a hell of a lot of thought since he and Claire and Sherry had stumbled away from the burning city, and the only real reason he could come up with was so stupid that he didn't want to credit it. Standing against Umbrella was the right thing to do—it was that he didn't feel *qualified* to be there.

Yep, that's pretty stupid.

Maybe it was—but it was holding him back, making him feel uncertain, and he needed to examine it.

David Trapp had made a career of the S.T.A.R.S., only to watch the organization fall under the control of Umbrella; he'd lost two close friends on a mission to infiltrate a bioweapons testing facility, as had John Andrews. Rebecca Chambers had just been starting out in the S.T.A.R.S., but she was some kind of scientific child prodigy with a deep interest in Umbrella's work; that and the fact that she'd been through more than anyone else made her continued dedication understandable. Claire wanted to find her brother, the only family she had; their parents were dead, and the two of them were close. Chris, Jill, and Barry he'd never met, but he was sure they had compelling reasons of their own; he knew Barry Burton's wife and children had been threatened, Rebecca had mentioned it...

And what about Leon Kennedy? He'd stumbled into the fight without a clue, a cop fresh out of the academy on his way to his first day at work—which just happened to be with the Raccoon PD. There was Ada, true—but he'd known her less than half a day, and she had been killed just after admitting to him that she was some kind of an agent, sent to steal a sample of an Umbrella virus.

So I lost a job, and a possible relationship with a woman I barely knew and couldn't trust. Of course Umbrella should be stopped... but do I belong here? He'd decided to become a cop because he wanted to help people, but he'd always figured that meant keeping the peace—busting drunk drivers, breaking up bar fights, catching crooks. Never in his wildest dreams would he have figured on being caught up in an international conspiracy, cloak-and-dagger infiltration-type stuff against a giant company that made war monsters. It was crime on a much bigger scale than he felt he was ready for...

...and is that the real reason, Officer Kennedy?

At exactly that moment, Claire mumbled something from her light doze, nuzzling her head against his arm before falling silent and still again—and making Leon uncomfortably aware of another facet to his involvement with the ex-S.T.A.R.S. Claire. Claire was... she was an incredible woman. In the days after their escape from Raccoon City, they'd talked a lot about what had happened, the experiences they'd had both separately and together. At the time, it had felt like an exchange of information, filling in blanks— she'd told him about her run-in with Chief Irons and the creature she'd called Mr. X, and he'd told her all about Ada and the terrible *thing* that had once been William Birkin. Between them, they'd been able to come up with a continuous story, with information that was important to the fugitive team.

In retrospect, though, he could see that those

long, rambling conversations had been essential for another reason entirely—they'd been a way to leach out the poison of what had happened to them, like talking out a bad dream. If he'd had to keep it all inside, he thought, he might have gone crazy.

In any case, the feelings he had for her now were convoluted ones—warmth, connection, dependence, respect, others that he had no name for. And that scared him, because he'd never felt so strongly about anyone before—and because he wasn't sure how much of it was real and how much was just some kind of a post-traumatic stress thing.

Face it, stop bullshitting yourself. What you're really afraid of is that you're only here because she is, and you don't like what that says about you.

Leon nodded inwardly, realizing that it was the truth, the real reason behind his uncertainty. He'd always believed that *want* was okay, but *need*? He didn't like the idea of being led around by some neurotic compulsion to be close to Claire Redfield.

And what if it isn't need? Maybe it's want, and you just don't know it yet...

He scowled at his own pathetic attempts at self-analysis, deciding that maybe it would be best just to stop worrying about it so much. Whatever the reason for becoming involved, he *was* involved—he could kick ass with the best of them and Umbrella deserved to have their ass kicked, big time. For now, he had to pee, and then he was going to eat something and do his best to catch some sleep.

Leon gently moved out from beneath Claire's warm, heavy head, doing his best not to wake her up. He slid out into the aisle, glancing around at the others. Rebecca was staring out her window, John was flipping through a muscle mag, David was dozing. They were all good people, and thinking that made him feel a little easier about things.

They're the good guys. Hell, I'm *a good guy, fighting for truth, justice, and fewer viral zombies in the world...*

The bathroom was in the front. Leon started toward it, steadying himself by touching each seat as he passed, thinking that the steady drone of the plane's engine was a soothing sound, like a waterfall—

—and then the curtain at the front of the cabin was pushed open, and a man stepped out, a tall, smiling man in an expensive-looking trench coat. He wasn't the pilot, and there wasn't anyone else on the plane, and Leon felt his mouth go dry with an almost superstitious dread even though the thin, smiling man didn't seem to be armed.

"Hey!" Leon shouted, backing up a step. "Hey, we got company!"

The man grinned, his eyes twinkling. "Leon Kennedy, I presume," he said softly, and Leon was suddenly absolutely sure that whoever he was, this man was trouble with a capital "T."

THREE

John was on his feet before Leon had finished his warning, hopping out into the aisle and stepping in front of Leon in a single stride.

"Who the hell—" John snarled, his shoulders set, ready to break the thin man in two if he so much as blinked wrong.

The stranger held up pale, long-fingered hands, looking as though he could barely contain his delight— which made John all the more wary. He could easily pound the guy into hamburger, what the hell was he so *happy* about?

"And you're John Andrews," the man said, his voice low and calm and as pleased as his expression. "Formerly a communications expert and field scout for the Exeter S.T.A.R.S. It's so good to meet you—tell me, how are your ribs? Still tender?"

Shit. Who is this guy? John had broken two ribs and cracked a third on the cove mission, and didn't know this man—how the hell did this man know *him?*

"My name is Trent," the stranger said easily, nodding at both Leon and John. "I believe your Mr. Trapp can vouch for my identity...?"

John flicked a glance back, saw that David and the girls were right behind them. David gave a quick nod, his expression strained.

Trent. Goddamn. The mysterious Mr. Trent.

—The same Mr. Trent who had given maps and clues to Jill Valentine, just before the Raccoon S.T.A.R.S. had discovered Umbrella's initial T-Virus spill at the Spencer estate. The Trent who had given a similar package to David one rainy August night, information about Umbrella's Caliban Cove facility, where Steve and Karen had been murdered.

The Trent who'd been playing games with the S.T.A.R.S.—with people's *lives*—all along.

Trent was still smiling, still holding his hands up. John noticed a black ring made out of stone on one slender finger, the only affectation that Mr. Trent seemed to have; it looked heavy and expensive.

"So what the hell do you want?" John growled. He didn't like secrets or surprises, and he didn't like the fact that Trent seemed totally unimpressed by his formidable size. Most people backed down when he got in their face; Trent seemed amused.

"Mr. Andrews, if you please... ?"

John didn't move, glaring into Trent's dark, intelligent eyes. Trent gazed back impassively, and John could see cool self-assurance in that bright gaze, a look that was almost but not quite patronizing. As big and buff as John was, he wasn't a violent man— but that confident, mirthful look made John think that Mr. Trent could use a good beating. Not by him, necessarily, but by *someone*.

How many people have died, just because he decided to stir things up a little?

"It's alright, John," David said quietly. "I'm sure that if Mr. Trent meant us harm, he wouldn't be standing here introducing himself."

David was right, whether John liked it or not. He sighed inwardly and stepped aside, but decided that he definitely didn't like it; from what little he knew about the man, he didn't like it at *all*.

Gonna be watching you, "friend"...

Trent nodded as though there had never been any question and walked past John, smiling at all of them. He motioned for them to sit in the seats on one side of the cabin; he took off his trench coat and put it aside, moving slowly and carefully, obviously aware that any sudden moves could be detrimental to his health. Beneath the coat he wore a black suit, black tie, and shoes; John didn't know clothes but the shoes were Asante. Trent had taste, anyway, and a shitload of money if he could afford to blow a couple thou on footwear.

"This may take a few moments," he said. "Please, get comfortable." He pushed himself up to sit atop one of the chairs opposite their group, moving with a smooth grace that made John feel even less comfortable. He moved like someone with training, martial arts maybe...

The others sat or leaned against the chairs, each of them studying the uninvited guest, each looking as unhappy about his appearance as John felt. Trent studied them in turn.

"Mr. Andrews, Mr. Kennedy, Mr. Trapp, and I have already met..." Trent looked back and forth between Rebecca and Claire, his sparkling gaze finally settling on Claire.

"Claire Redfield, yes?" He seemed a little more hesitant, which wasn't a surprise. Rebecca and Claire could have been sisters, both brunettes, same height, only a few months difference in age.

"Yes," Claire said. "Does the pilot know you're on board?"

John frowned, irritated with himself for not having asked first. It was a fairly important question, and it hadn't occurred to him. If the pilot had let Mr. Trent aboard...

Trent nodded, running one pale hand through his tousled black hair. "Yes, he does. In fact, Captain Evans is an acquaintance of mine, so when I realized that you were going... traveling, I arranged for him to be in the right place at the right time. Much easier than it sounds, really."

"Why?" David asked, an edge coming into his voice that John had only ever heard in combat situations. The captain was right on the verge of being seriously upset. "Why would you do that, Mr. Trent?"

Trent seemed to ignore him. "I realize that you're concerned about your friends on the Continent, but let me assure you that they're in the best of health. Really, there's no reason for you to worry yourselves—"

"*Why?*" David's voice was steel.

Trent stared at him, then sighed. "Because I don't want you to go to Europe, and making it so that Captain Evans is your pilot means that you won't. You can't. In fact, we should be turning back any moment now."

* * *

Claire stared at him, feeling her stomach knot, feeling that knot transforming into a burning, leaden anger.

Chris, I won't see Chris—

John pushed away from the seat he'd been leaning on and grabbed Trent's arm before Claire could even open her mouth, before anyone had time to respond to his statement.

"Tell your 'acquaintance' to keep right on goin' the way we're goin'," John spat, glowering at Trent. From the way John's hands were shaking, Claire thought there was a good chance that he would break Trent's arm—and found that she didn't think that was such a bad idea.

Trent wore an expression of mild discomfort, nothing more. "I'm sorry to interrupt your plans," he said, "but if you'll hear me out, I think you'll agree that it's for the best—if you really want to stop Umbrella, that is."

For the best? Chris, we have to help Chris and the others, what is this shit?

She waited for the others to explode into action, to storm the cockpit, to tie Mr. Trent to a chair and force him to explain himself—but they were all silent, looking at one another and at Trent with shock, anger—and interest, guarded but interest nonetheless. John loosened his grip, glancing at David for direction.

"This had better be a good story, Mr. Trent," David said coolly. "I'm aware that you've—helped us in the past, but this kind of interference isn't the kind of help we want or need."

He tipped his head at John, who reluctantly let go of Trent and stepped back. Not very far back, Claire noticed.

If Trent had been worried at all, there was no sign of it. He nodded at David, and in his low, musical voice, started to speak.

"As I'm sure you're all aware, Umbrella, Inc., has facilities in locations all around the world, factories and plants that employ thousands of people and generate hundreds of millions of dollars each year. Most of them are legitimate pharmaceutical or chemical companies, and have no relevance to this discussion, except that they're quite profitable; the money generated by Umbrella's legal enterprises allows them to finance their lesser-known operations—operations that you and yours have recently had the misfortune to come across.

"These operations fall into a division known as

White Umbrella, and most have to do with bioweapons research. There are very few who know all of the ins and outs of White Umbrella's business, but the ones who do are extremely powerful. Powerful, and committed to creating all sorts of unpleasantness. Chemical weapons, fatal diseases... the T and G series viruses that have been so troublesome as of late."

That's *an understatement*, Claire thought nastily, but was intrigued in spite of herself. To finally *know* something about what they were up against...

"Why?" Leon asked. "Chemical warfare isn't all that profitable, anyone with a centrifuge and some gardening supplies can come up with a bioweapon."

Rebecca was nodding. "And the kind of work they're doing, applying rapid fuse virions to genetic redistribution—it's incredibly expensive, and as hazardous to work with as nuclear waste. Worse."

Trent shook his head. "They're doing it because they can. Because they want to." He smiled faintly. "Because when you're richer and more powerful than anyone else on the planet, you get bored."

"Who gets bored?" David asked.

Trent gazed at him for a moment, then started talking again, blatantly ignoring David's question. "White Umbrella's current focus is on bio-organic soldiers, if you will—individual specimens, most genetically altered, all injected with some variation of virus intended to make them violent and strong and oblivious to pain. The manner in which these viruses amplify in humans, the 'zombie' reaction, is nothing more than an unexpected side effect; the viruses Umbrella creates are designed for nonhuman use, at least at this point."

Claire was interested, but she was also getting impatient. "So when do we get to the part about why you're here, why you don't want us going to Europe?" she asked, not bothering to keep the anger out of her voice.

Trent looked at her, his dark eyes suddenly sympathetic, and she realized that he knew why she was angry, that he knew all about her reasons for wanting to go to Europe. She could see it in the way he gazed at her, his eyes telling her that he understood— and she suddenly felt deeply uneasy.

He knows everything, doesn't he? All about us...

"Not all of the White Umbrella facilities are the same," he continued. "There are some that deal strictly with data, some only with the chemistry, some where specimens are grown or surgically pieced together—and a very few where these specimens are tested. And that brings us to why I'm here, and why I'd rather you postponed your plans.

"There's an Umbrella testing facility about to go on line in Utah, just north of the salt flats. Right now, it's staffed by a very small crew of technicians and... specimen handlers, and is scheduled to become fully operational in about three weeks. The man overseeing the final preparations is one of White Umbrella's key players, a man named Reston. The job was supposed to have been handled by another fellow, a despicable little man by the name of Lewis, but Mr. Lewis had an unfortunate and not entirely unplanned accident... and now Reston is in charge. And because he is one of the very important men behind White Umbrella, he has, in his possession, a little black book. There are only three of these books, and the other two would be nearly impossible to get hold of..."

"So what's in it?" John snapped. "Get to the point."

Trent smiled at John as if he had asked politely. "Each book is a kind of master key; each has a complete directory of codes used to program every mainframe in every White Umbrella facility. With that book, one could conceivably break into any lab or test site and access everything from personnel files to financial statements. They'll change the codes once the book is stolen, of course—but unless they want to lose everything they've stored, it will take them months."

No one spoke for a moment, the only sound that of the plane's insistent hum. Claire looked at each of them, saw the thoughtful expressions, saw that they were seriously considering Trent's implied proposal— and realized that it had just become highly unlikely that they would be going to Europe after all.

* * *

"But what about Chris, and Jill and Barry? You said they were okay—how do you know that?" Claire asked, and David could just hear the barely hidden desperation.

"It would take a very long time to explain how I come by my information," Trent said smoothly. "And while I'm certain you don't want to hear this, I'm afraid you'll just have to trust me. Your brother and his companions are in no immediate danger, they don't need you at the moment—but the opportunity to get Reston's book, to get into that lab, will be gone in less than a week. There's no security detail right now, half the systems aren't even running—and as long as you stay away from the test program, there are no creatures to contend with."

David wasn't sure what to think. It sounded good, it sounded like exactly the opportunity they'd been hoping for... but then, so had Caliban Cove. So had a lot of things.

And as for trusting Mr. Trent...

"What's your stake in this?" David asked. "Why do you want to hurt Umbrella?"

Trent shrugged. "Call it a hobby."

"I'm serious," David said.

"So am I." Trent smiled, his eyes still dancing with that twinkling humor. David had only seen him once before, hadn't exchanged more than a dozen words, but Trent seemed just as strangely happy now as he had then; whatever it was that made him tick, it was certainly bringing him a lot of pleasure.

"Why have you been so cryptic?" Rebecca asked, and David nodded, saw that the others were doing the same. "The stuff you gave to Jill, and to David, before—all riddles and clues. Why not just tell us what we need to know?"

"Because you needed to figure it out," Trent said. "Or, rather, it was necessary that you *appeared* to figure it out, all by yourselves. As I said before, there are very few people who know what White Umbrella is doing; if you seemed to know too much, it might come back to me."

"Then why take the risk now?" David asked. "For that matter, why do you need us at all? You obviously have some connection to White Umbrella; why not go public, or sabotage them from the inside?"

Trent smiled again. "I'm taking the risk because it's time to take a risk. And as to the rest... all I can say is that I have my reasons."

He talks and talks, and yet we still don't know what the hell he's doing, or why... how exactly does he manage that?

"Why don't you tell us a few of those reasons, Trent?" None of it was sitting well with John, David saw; he was scowling at their stowaway, looking as though he might have to be talked out of punching the man.

Trent didn't answer. Instead, he pushed himself off of the seat and picked up his coat, turning to look at David.

"I realize you'll want to discuss this before you make your decision," he said. "If you'll excuse me, I'll take this opportunity to visit our captain. If you decide against collecting Reston's book, I'll step aside. I said before that you had no choice, but that was my dramatic side showing, I suppose; there's always a choice."

On that, Trent turned and walked to the front of the cabin and slipped behind the curtain without a backward glance.

FOUR

John broke the silence about two seconds after Trent left the cabin.

"To hell with this," he said, looking as pissed off as Rebecca had ever seen him. "I don't know about the rest of you, but I'm not all that happy about being played like this—I'm not here to be Mr. Trent's boy, and I don't trust him. I say we get him to talk about Umbrella, tell us what he knows about our team in Europe—and if he gives us one more say-nothing answer, we should drop-kick his evasive ass out the damned door."

Rebecca knew he was royally ticked, but she couldn't help herself. "Yeah, John, but how do you *really* feel?"

He glared in her direction—and then grinned, and somehow, that broke the tension for all of them. It was as though they all remembered how to breathe again at the same time; the unexpected visit from their mysterious benefactor had made it hard for a few moments to remember much of anything.

"We've got John's vote," David said. "Claire? I know you were worried about Chris..."

Claire nodded slowly. "Yeah. And I want to see him again, as soon as possible..."

"But," David said, coaxing the rest of it out.

"But—I think he's telling the truth. About them being okay, I mean."

Leon was nodding. "I do, too. John's right about him being slick—but I don't think he was lying, about anything. He didn't tell us a lot, but I didn't get the impression that he was bullshitting us with what he *would* say."

David turned toward her. "Rebecca?"

She sighed, shaking her head. "Sorry, John, but I agree. I think he's got some credibility; he's helped us before, in his own weird way, and the fact that he's here, unarmed, says something—"

"—it says he's a dumbass," John muttered darkly, and Rebecca punched him lightly on the arm, realizing suddenly, intuitively, why John was so reluctant to accept Trent's word.

Trent wasn't intimidated by him.

She was sure of it; she knew John well enough to know that Trent's indifference would absolutely push his buttons.

Choosing her words carefully, keeping her tone light, Rebecca grinned at him. "I think you just hate the fact that he's not scared of your big scary self,

John. Most people would've wet their pants with you towering over them."

It was the right thing to say. John frowned thoughtfully, then shrugged. "Yeah, well, maybe. I still don't trust him, though."

"I don't think any of us should," David said. "He's keeping an awful lot to himself for someone who wants our help. The question is, do we seek out this Reston, or do we continue with our original plans?"

No one spoke for a moment, and Rebecca could see that no one wanted to say it—to acknowledge that if Trent was telling the truth, there was no reason to go to Europe. She didn't want to say it, either; somehow, it felt like a betrayal of Jill and Chris and Barry, like, "we've found something better to do than come to your aid."

But if they don't need us...

Rebecca decided that she may as well go first. "If this place is as easy as he says... when would we ever have another chance like this?"

Claire was biting at her lip, looking unhappy. Looking *torn.* "If we found that book of codes, we'd have something to take with us to Europe. Something that could really make a difference."

"*If* we find the book," John said, but Rebecca could see that the idea was growing on him.

"It could be a turning point," David said softly. "It would knock the odds against us down from a million to one to perhaps only a few thousand."

"I have to admit, it would be fine to turn over

Umbrella's private files to the press," John said. "Download all of their shitty little secrets and pass them out to every paper in the country."

They were all nodding, and although she thought it might take a little more time to get used to the idea, Rebecca knew that the decision had been made.

It seemed that they were going to Utah.

* * *

If anyone had expected Trent to be overjoyed at the news, they would have been deeply disappointed. When David called him back to the cabin and told him that they would go to the new testing facility, Trent only nodded, that same enigmatic smile on his lined and weathered face.

"Here are the coordinates for the site," Trent said, pulling a slip of paper from his front pocket. "There are also several numerical codes listed, one of which will provide entry—although the keypad may be hard to find. I'm sorry I wasn't able to narrow it down any further."

Leon watched as David took the paper from Trent, as Trent walked back out to tell the pilot, wondering why it was that he couldn't stop thinking about Ada. Since Trent's little speech about White Umbrella, memories of Ada Wong's skill and beauty, echoes of her deep, sultry voice had been haunting Leon. It wasn't a conscious thing, or at least not at first. It was that something about the man reminded him of her; maybe that supreme self-confidence, or that hint of sly smile—

—and at the end, before that crazy woman shot her, I accused her of being an Umbrella spy—and she'd said that she wasn't, that who she worked for wasn't my concern...

Although he and Claire had come into the fight pretty late in the game, they'd been thoroughly briefed on what the others knew about Umbrella, and what part Trent had played in the past. The one constant—besides being incredibly elusive with information—was that he seemed to know all sorts of things that no one else knew.

It can't hurt to ask.

When Trent walked back into the cabin, Leon approached him.

"Mr. Trent," he said carefully, watching him closely, "in Raccoon City, I met a woman named Ada Wong..."

Trent gazed at him, his face giving nothing away. "Yes?"

"I was wondering if you knew anything about her, about who she was working for. She was looking for a sample of the G-Virus—"

Trent arched his eyebrows. "Was she? And did she find it?"

Leon studied his dark, quick eyes, wondering why he felt like Trent already knew the answer. He couldn't, of course, Ada had been murdered just before the laboratory had exploded.

"Yes, she did," Leon said. "In the end, though, she—she sacrificed herself in a way, rather than make a choice. Between killing someone and losing the sample."

"And was that someone you?" Trent asked softly.

Leon was aware that the others were watching, and was a little surprised that he wasn't at all uncomfortable. Even a month ago, such a personal conversation would have been embarrassing for him.

"Yeah," he said, almost defiantly. "It was me."

Trent nodded slowly, smiling a little. "Then it seems to me that you wouldn't need to know anything else about her. About her character or motivations."

Leon wasn't sure if he was evading the question or honestly telling him what he thought—but either way, the simple logic of his answer made Leon feel better. As though he'd known the answer himself all along. Whatever psychology he was working, Trent was quite a piece of work.

He's smooth, cultured, and scary as hell in his own quiet way...Ada would have liked him.

"...much as I'd enjoy talking with you, I have some business with our captain that needs to be attended to," Trent was saying. "We'll be at Salt Lake in five or six hours."

With that, he nodded toward them and disappeared through the curtain again.

"Too good to sit with the grunts?" John asked, obviously not over his initial dislike. Leon looked around at the others, saw thoughtful and uneasy expressions, saw Claire looking as though she half wanted to change her mind.

Leon walked to where she was leaning against a seat, her arms folded tightly, and touched her shoulder.

"Thinking about Chris?" He asked gently.

To his surprise, she shook her head, smiling at him nervously. "No. Actually, I was thinking about the Spencer estate, and the raid on Caliban Cove, and what happened in Raccoon. I was thinking that no matter what Trent says about how simple this will be, nothing is ever simple with Umbrella. Things have a way of getting complicated when they're involved. You'd think we would know that by now..."

She trailed off, then shook her head as if trying to clear it, giving him another, brighter smile. "Listen to me talk. I'm going to get a sandwich, you want anything?"

"No, thanks," he said absently, still thinking about what she'd said as she walked away—and wondering suddenly if their little trek to Utah was going to be the last mistake that any of them ever made.

* * *

Steve Lopez, good ol' Steve, his face as blank and white as a sheet of paper, standing in the middle of the strange, vast laboratory, standing and aiming his semi at them and telling them to drop their weapons—

—and the rage, the pain and red fury that hit John like a hurricane as he realized what had happened, that Karen was dead, that Steve had been turned into one of those crazy asshole's zombie soldiers—

—and John screamed, what did you do to him, not thinking, spinning instead, firing at the blank-faced drone behind them, the round punching neatly through its left temple and the cold air stinking like death as the creature fell—

—and pain! Pain, tearing through him as Steve, Stevie, his friend and comrade, shot him in the back. John felt blood dribble from his lips, felt himself turning, felt more pain than he thought he could feel. Steve had shot him, the mad doctor had used the virus on him and Steve wasn't Steve anymore and the world was spinning, screaming—

John, John wake up you're having

"—a bad dream. Hey, big guy—"

John sat up, his eyes wide and his heart thumping, feeling disoriented and afraid. The cool hand on his arm was Rebecca's, the touch gentle and soothing, and he realized that he was awake, that he'd been dreaming and was now awake.

"Shit," he mumbled, and sagged back against his seat, closing his eyes. They were still on the plane, the soft drone of the engine and the hiss of canned air putting to rest the last of his confusion.

"You okay?" Rebecca asked, and John nodded, taking a few deep breaths before he opened his eyes again.

"Did I—did I yell or anything?"

Rebecca smiled at him, watching him closely. "Nope. Just so happens I was on my way back from the bathroom and saw you twitching like a rabbit. It didn't look like you were having much fun... hope I didn't interrupt anything good."

The last was almost a question. John forced a grin and avoided the subject entirely, glancing out at the passing darkness instead. "Three tuna sandwiches before bed was a bad idea, I guess. We almost there?"

Rebecca nodded. "We're just starting the descent. Fifteen, twenty minutes, David says."

She was still scrutinizing him, still wearing an expression of warmth and concern, and John realized he was being an idiot. Keeping that shit to oneself was a sure ticket to losing one's mind.

"I was in the lab," he said, and Rebecca nodded, it was all he needed to say. She'd been there.

"I had one just a couple of days ago, right after we decided to leave Exeter," she said softly. "A real nasty one. It was kind of a combination, stuff from the Spencer lab and from the cove."

John nodded, thinking about what a remarkable young woman she was. She'd faced down a houseful of Umbrella monsters on her first S.T.A.R.S. mission, and had still decided to come with them to check out the cove when David had asked.

"You kick ass, 'becca. If I were a few years younger, I think it might be love," he said, and was pleased at her blushing, grinning reaction. She was probably smarter than him by half, but she was also a teenage girl—and if he remembered correctly from back in his day, teenage girls weren't adverse to hearing about how cool they were.

"Shut up," she said, her tone of voice telling him that he had, in fact, thoroughly embarrassed her— and that she didn't mind.

A moment of comfortable silence rested between them, the last dregs of the nightmare fading as the cabin pressure fluctuated, the plane on its way down. In a few minutes, they'd be in Utah, of all places. David had already suggested that they get to a hotel and start making plans, that they would go in tomorrow night.

Go in, get the book, and then get the hell out. Easy... except hadn't that pretty much been the plan for the cove?

John decided that once they landed, he wanted to do a little more talking with Trent. He was up for the mission, for getting the book and throwing a few wrenches into Umbrella's works in the process—but he still wasn't happy with Trent's rather selective information. Yeah, the man was helping them— but why so weird about it? And why hadn't he told them what their Europe team was doing, or who was running White Umbrella, or how he'd known to put his own pilot on their charter?

Because he's on some power trip, that's why. Control freak.

That didn't seem quite right, but John couldn't think of any other reason that their Mr. Trent was being such a secret agent wannabe spy. Maybe if he got his arm twisted a little, he'd be more forthcoming...

"John—I know you don't like him, but do you think

he's right about this being a snap job? I mean, what if this Reston won't give it up? Or what if—what if something else happens?"

She was trying to sound professional, her tone light and easy, but the troubled look deep in her mild brown eyes gave her away.

Something else. Something like a viral spill, something like a crazy scientist, something like biomonsters getting loose. Like the something that always happens around Umbrella...

"If I have anything to say about it, the only thing that will go wrong is that Reston will shit himself and the smell will be terrible," he said, and was again rewarded with a grin from the young woman.

"You're a dork," she said, and John shrugged, thinking how easy it was to make the girl smile—and wondering if it was such a good idea to get her hopes up.

A few moments later the small plane touched down easily and for the first time, the pilot used the intercom system. He told them to remain seated until the plane had stopped and then clicked off, not bothering with the usual crap about how he hoped they'd enjoyed their flight or what the current temperature was; for that, at least, John was grateful. The small craft rolled across the tarmac, finally coming to a gentle stop, the team standing and stretching and putting on their coats.

As soon as he heard the outer door pop, John stepped past Rebecca and walked to the front of the cabin, determined not to let Trent get off before they'd had a chance to chat. He pushed through the curtain, a cold wind blowing into the small passage behind the cockpit, and saw that he was too late. The pilot, Evans, was standing in the doorway to the cockpit by himself.

Somehow, Trent had managed to slip away in the few seconds it took John to walk through the tiny plane. The metal stairs that had been pushed to the outside of the craft were empty—and even though John took the steps two at a time, hitting the ground in less than a heartbeat, there was still nothing to see in the endless stretch of tarmac, and no one at all except for the man who'd brought the stairs out. When asked about Trent, the airport worker insisted that the first person off the plane had been John himself.

"Son of a bitch," John spat, and it didn't matter, because they were in Utah. Trent or no Trent, they had arrived—and because it was after midnight, they had less than a day to get ready.

FIVE

Jay Reston was pleased. In fact, he was as happy as he'd been in a long time, and if he'd known it would feel so good to be back in the field, he would have done it years ago.

Managing employees, the kind who actually get their hands dirty. Making things happen and seeing the results unfold, being a part of the process. Being more than just a shadow, more than some nameless darkness to be feared...

Thinking these things made him feel strong and vital again; he was barely fifty, he hadn't yet come to see himself as even middle-aged, but working in the trenches again made him realize how much he'd lost over the years.

Reston sat in the control room, the pulse of the Planet, his hands behind his head and his attention fixed on the wall of screens in front of him. On one screen, a man in coveralls was working on a series of trees in Phase One, adding another coat of green to a row of faux evergreens. The man was Tom Something-or-other, from construction, but the name wasn't important. What *was* important was that Tom was painting the trees because Reston had told him to, face-to-face at the morning briefing.

On another screen, Kelly McMalus was recalibrating the desert temp control, also at Reston's request. McMalus was the Scorps lead handler, at least until the permanent staff came in; everyone in the Planet was temporary, one of White's newer policies to avoid sabotage. Once everything was up and running, the nine technical people and half-dozen "preliminary" researchers—actually glorified specimen handlers, although he'd never call them that directly—would be relocated.

The Planet. The facility was actually "B.O.W. Envirotest A," but Reston thought that Planet was a much better name. He wasn't sure who had come up with it, just that it had cropped up at one of the morning briefings and stuck. Referring to the test site as the Planet in his updates to the home team made him feel even more a part of the process.

"The video feeds were connected today, although there's some problem with the mikes, so the audio hasn't been hooked up yet; I'll have that taken care of ASAP. The last of the Ma3Ks came in, no damage to any of the specimens. In all, things are going very well, we expect to have the Planet ready days ahead of schedule..."

Reston smiled, thinking of his last conversation with Sidney; had he heard just a touch of jealousy in Sidney's voice, a thread of wistfulness? He was part of a "we" now, a we that called Envirotest A by a nickname. After thirty years of delegation, having to oversee the finishing touches on their most innovative and expensive facility to date had been a blessing in disguise. And to think that he'd been irritated when he'd first heard about Lewis's car going off a cliff; the man's accident was probably the best work he'd ever done for Umbrella, because it meant that he would be overseeing the Planet's birth.

Another tech was walking across one of the screens, carrying a tool box and a coil of rope. Cole, Henry Cole, the electrician who'd been working on the intercom and video systems; he was in the main corridor that ran between the faculty quarters and the testing area, leading toward the elevator. Reston had noticed the day before that several of the surface cameras were malfunctioning; none of the cameras in the Planet had been wired for sound as of yet, but the screens for the upper compound would intermittently spew static for minutes at a time, and he had asked Cole to see to it—

—but after he'd finished with the 'com system, not before. How am I supposed to stay in contact with these people if I don't have a working intercom system?

Even the flush of irritation he felt for the tech was exhilarating; instead of pushing a button, telling some yes-man to fix it, he would have to attend to it himself.

Reston pushed away from the console, stretching as he stood up, taking a last look at the row of monitors to remind him of anything else he needed to see to as long as he was out.

Intercom, video feeds... the bridge in Three will need reinforcement, that's not a priority, but we really should do something about the city colors, they're still much too flat...

He walked through the sleekly designed control room, past the line of plush leather chairs so new that their rich scent still lingered in the cool filtered air. The chairs faced a wall of high-resolution screens; in less than a month they would be seating the top researchers, scientists, and administrators that were the heart of White Umbrella, as well as the two biggest financiers of the program. Even Sidney and Jackson would be there, to see the initial run of the test program.

And Trent, Reston thought hopefully. *Surely he wouldn't turn down an invitation to the first test run...*

Reston stepped on the pressure plate in front of the door, the thick metal hatch sliding up with only a whisper of sound, and walked out into the wide corridor that ran the length of the Planet. Control wasn't far from the industrial elevator, almost straight across in fact, but the electrician had already started for the surface. There would be four lifts operating within the week out of one of the other surface buildings, but for now, there was only the one industrial elevator. He'd have to wait until Cole had exited.

He pushed the recall and straightened the cuffs of his suit jacket, thinking about how he would lead the tour. It had been quite a while since Jay Reston had indulged in daydreaming, but in his short time at the Planet, imagining the day when he would welcome the others and guide them through the facility he had managed and transformed into a smoothly running machine had become a favored pastime. Of the handful of people who ran White Umbrella, who made the big decisions, he was the youngest to be accepted into the inner circle—and while Jackson had often assured him that he was as valued as anyone else, he'd noted on more than one occasion that he was the last to be consulted. To be *considered*.

Not after this. Not after they see that even without a dozen assistants waiting on my every word, I've managed to get the Planet up and running without a hitch, and before schedule. I'd like to see Sidney do half as well...

They'd come in at night, of course, and probably in several groups. He'd have the specimen caretakers at the entrance to greet them and lead them to the elevators (the new ones, not the dirty monstrosity he was about to ride); on the way down, the visitors would hear all about the efficient, elegant living quarters, the self-contained air-filtering system, the surgical theater—everything that made the Planet their most brilliant innovation yet. From the elevators, he'd take them around to the control room and explain the environments and the current series of specimens, eight of each. Then, back out and north, toward the beginning of the testing site.

We walk straight through, all four phases, then view autopsy and the chemical lab. We'll have to stop in for a look at Fossil, of course, and then through the living area—where there will be coffee and rolls, sandwiches maybe—and then circle back to control to observe the first tests. Specimen against specimen only, of course— human experimentation would put such a damper on things...

A soft tone brought his attention back to the errand, alerting him to the elevator's return. The door opened, the gate slid aside, and Reston stepped into the large car, the reinforced steel platform clanking beneath his feet. Dust puffed up from the metal, settling over the polished sheen of his shoes.

Reston sighed, tapping the controls that would take him to the surface, thinking of all he'd had to put up with since arriving at the Planet only ten days before. Things *were* coming along, but he'd never realized just how many inconveniences one had to suffer to get one of these places operational—the lukewarm meals, the constant need to pay attention to every niggling detail, and the *dirt*: everywhere, thin layers of workman's dust clung to hair and clothes, clogging the filters... even in the control room, he'd had to take all kinds of extra precautions to keep it from getting into the central terminal. He'd had to work with three different programmers to get the mainframe running, yet another of Umbrella's precautions to keep any one of them from knowing too much; but if the system were to go down...

Reston sighed again, patting the small, flat square in his inner pocket as the lift hummed smoothly upwards. He had the codes; if the system went down, he'd just have to call in new programmers. A setback, but hardly a disaster. Raccoon City, now *that* was a disaster—and all the more reason that he wanted things to go well with the Planet.

We need this. After the summer we've had, the spill and those meddling S.T.A.R.S. and losing Birkin... I need this.

Although it had been a unanimous decision, it had been Reston's people who'd gone into Raccoon to take Birkin's G-Virus—an action that had resulted in the loss of their lead scientist and just over a billion dollars' worth of equipment, space, and manpower. It wasn't his fault, of course, no one blamed him—but it had been a bad summer for all of them, and having Envirotest A up and running would ease things considerably.

He thought about what Trent had said, just before Reston had left for the Planet—that as long as they didn't lose their heads, there was no need for concern. Generic placating advice, but hearing it from Trent made it sound like the truth. It was funny; they'd brought Trent in to act as trouble shooter, and in less than six months he'd become one of the most respected members of their circle. Nothing rattled Trent, the man was ice; they were lucky to have him, particularly considering their recent run of misfortune.

The elevator came to a stop and Reston squared his shoulders, preparing himself to redirect Mr. Cole's efforts—and just the thought of making the man jump made him smile again, all other worries put aside for the moment.

Just a working-class Joe, he thought happily, and stepped out to take care of business.

SIX

There was a half-moon in the clear night sky, casting a pallid blue light across the vast, open stretch of plain and making it seem even colder than it was.

And that's pretty goddamn cold, Claire thought, shivering in spite of the rental's blasting heater. It was another minivan, and even with the three of them moving around in the back, checking weapons and loading clips, they didn't seem to be generating nearly enough heat to ward off the icy air that seeped in through the thin metal shell.

"Do you have the 380s?" John asked Leon, who handed over the box of rounds before going back to loading up their hip packs. David was driving, Rebecca checking their position on a GPS. If Trent's coordinates were correct, they'd be getting close.

Claire looked out at the pale landscape passing by the dirt track, the seemingly endless miles of nothing beneath the wide open sky, and shivered again. It was a barren, forsaken place, the road they were on scarcely more that a dirt track leading in from nowhere; a perfect setting for Umbrella.

The plan was simple. Park the van a half mile or so from Trent's coordinates, load up with every weapon they had, and slip into the compound as quietly as they could manage...

"...we'll find this entry keypad of Trent's, run the codes through, and go in strong," David had said, "well after dark. With any luck, the majority of the workers will be asleep; just a matter of finding the staff quarters and rounding them up. We'll confine them and have a check around for this book of Mr. Reston's; John, you and Claire will keep watch over our captives, while the rest of us search. It would probably be in their operations room, or in Reston's private quarters. If we haven't found it within, say, twenty minutes, we'll have to ask Mr. Reston directly—a last resort, to avoid implicating Trent. Book in hand, we go back out the way we came in. Questions?"

Their planning session at the hotel had made it sound easy enough—and with as little information as they had, the questions had been few. Now, though, driving through an endless, freezing waste and trying to get psyched up for a confrontation—now it didn't seem so simple. It was a scary prospect, going into a place none of them had ever been before and trying to find an item no bigger than a paperback novel.

Plus it's Umbrella, plus we'll have to intimidate the crap out of a bunch of technicians and possibly end up having to strong-arm one of the big boys.

At least they were going in well armed; it seemed that they had learned something about dealing with Umbrella, after all—that taking in a shitload of firepower was a very good idea. In addition to the nine-millimeter handguns and multiple clips that each of them would carry, they had two M-16 Als, automatic rifles—one for John, one for David—and a half-dozen fragmentation hand grenades. Just in case, David said.

In case everything falls apart. In case we have to blow up some bizarre, murderous creature—or a hundred of them...

"Cold?" Leon asked.

Claire turned away from the window, looking at him. He'd finished with the packs, and was holding one out to her. She took it, nodding in response to his question. "Aren't you?"

He shook his head, grinning. "Thermal underwear. Could have used these in Raccoon..."

Claire smiled. "*You* could have used them? I was running around in a pair of shorts, you at least had your uniform."

"Which was covered with lizard guts before I was halfway through the sewers," he said, and she was glad to hear him at least try to joke about it.

He's getting better; we both are.

"Now, children," John said sternly. "If you don't stop, we're turning this car around—"

"Slow down," Rebecca said from the front, her

quiet voice stilling them. David let up on the gas, the van slowing to a crawl.

"It looks like—it's about a half-mile southeast from our current position," Rebecca said.

Claire took a deep breath, saw John pick up one of the rifles, and saw Leon's mouth press into a thin line as David brought the van to a stop. It was time. John opened the side door and the air was ice, dry and bitterly cold.

"Hope they got the coffee on," John breathed, and hopped out into the darkness, reaching back in to grab his pack. Rebecca loaded up a few medical supplies, and as she and David climbed out, Leon put his hand on Claire's shoulder.

"You up for this?" he asked softly, and Claire smiled inwardly, thinking of how sweet he was; she'd been thinking of asking him the same thing. In the days since Raccoon, they'd gotten pretty close—and although she wasn't positive, she'd picked up on a few signals that suggested he wouldn't mind getting closer. She still wasn't sure if that was a good idea—

—and now's not the time to be deciding. The sooner we get this code book, the sooner we get to Europe. To Chris.

"As up as I'm gonna be," she said, and Leon nodded, and they climbed out into the freezing night to join the others.

* * *

David put John at the rear and took the lead himself, forcing all negative thoughts out of his mind as they struck out for where Trent said the test site would be. It wasn't easy; they were going in cold with less than a day's planning, no layout, no idea what Reston looked like or what kind of security they'd be facing—

—the list is endless, isn't it, and I'm still taking them in. Because if we're successful, I can step down. Umbrella will be as good as dead and no one will have to look to me for anything, ever again.

That was a thought he could hold on to; a peaceful retirement. Once the monsters behind White Umbrella had been brought to justice, vigilante or otherwise, he'd have no greater responsibility than keeping himself fed and bathed. Perhaps he'd work up to a house-plant...

"I think—veer left a few degrees," Rebecca said from behind him, startling him, bringing his focus back around. She'd barely spoken above a whisper, but the night was so cold and crisp, the air so perfectly still that every step taken, every breath exhaled seemed to fill the world.

David led them through the darkness, wishing they could use their lights; they should be getting quite close. But even dressed all in black, he was worried they'd be spotted before they could get inside— whatever that meant exactly; Trent had given them no idea of what the facility would look like. In any case, with barely a half moon they wouldn't see it until they were right on top—

There.

A thickening of shadow, straight ahead. David held up his hand, slowing the others as they moved closer, as he saw a dented metal roof reflecting moonlight. And then a fence, and then a handful of buildings, all of them dark and silent.

David dropped into a walking crouch, motioning for the rest to follow suit, holding the automatic rifle tight against his chest. They crept closer, close enough to see the lonely group of tall one-story structures behind a low fence.

Five, six buildings, no lights, no movement—a front, surely...

"Underground," Rebecca whispered, and David nodded. Probably; they'd discussed several possibilities, and it seemed the most likely. Even in the wan light he could see that the buildings were old, dusty and worn. There was a smallish structure in the front, five long, low buildings in a row behind it, all with sloping metal roofs. It was certainly big enough to be some kind of a testing ground, the larger buildings as big as aircraft hangars, but between the site's placement—alone, out in the open in the middle of a desert—and the wear and tear, he'd guess underground.

Good and bad. Good, because they should be able to get into the compound without much trouble; bad because God only knew what kind of surveillance system had been set up. They would have to go in fast.

David turned, still in a crouch, and faced the team. "We'll need to double-time," he said softly, "and stay low. We scale the fence, head for the structure closest to the front gate, same order—I'm on point, John's in back. We have to find the entry ASAP. Watch for cameras, and everyone's armed as soon as we're in the compound."

Nods all around, faces grim and set. David turned and started for the fence, head down, his muscles tight and jumping. Twenty meters, the air biting into his lungs, freezing the light sweat on his skin. Ten meters. Five, and he could see the "No Trespassing" signs posted on the fence, and as they reached the gate, David saw the sign telling them that they were at the privately owned "Weather Monitoring and Survey #7." He looked up and saw the rounded silhouettes of what had to be satellite dishes on two of the buildings, plus the multiple thin lines of antennae stretching up from one of them.

David touched the fence with the barrel of the M-16, then with his hand. Nothing, and there was no barbed wire either, no sensor lines that he could see, no alarm trips.

Obviously, no weather station would have those; trust Umbrella to be as concise in their fronts as with anything else.

He slung the rifle over his shoulder, grabbed the thick wire and pulled himself up. It was only seven feet; he was at the top in five seconds, flipping himself over and jumping to the dusty ground inside the compound.

Rebecca was next, climbing quickly and easily, a

lithe shadow in the dark. David reached up to help her, but she leapt nimbly to the ground next to him with hardly a stumble. She drew her weapon, an H&K VP70, and turned to cover the darkness as David looked back to the fence.

Leon almost tripped off the top, but David managed to steady him, grabbing the younger man's hand; once he was down, he nodded his thanks at David and turned to help Claire over.

So far, so good...

David scanned the shadows around them as John scaled the outside, his heart pounding, all of his senses on high alert. There was no sound but the gentle *clank* of the fence, no movement in the blackness.

He glanced back as John thumped to the cold and dusty ground, then nodded toward the front structure, the smaller one. If he were to design a false cover, he'd hide the real entrance somewhere no one would look—in a broom closet at the back of the last building, through a trap door in the dirt—but Umbrella was cocky, too smug to worry about such simple precautions.

It will be in the first building, because they'll believe they've hidden it so cleverly that no one will find it. Because if there's one thing we can count on, it's that Umbrella thinks they're too smart to be caught out...

He hoped. Staying down, David started for the building, praying that if there were cameras watching them, there was no one watching the cameras.

* * *

It was late, but Reston wasn't tired. He sat in the control room, sipping brandy from a ceramic mug and idly thinking about the next day's agenda.

He'd make his report, of course; Cole still hadn't managed to fix the intercom system, although the video cameras all seemed to be in working order; the Ca6 handler, Les Duvall, wanted one of the mechanics to see about a sticking lock on the release cage—and there was still the city. The Ma3Ks couldn't exactly shine if the only colors were tan and brick...

...have to get the construction people into Four tomorrow. And see how the Avis do with the perches—

A red light flashed on the panel in front of him, accompanied by a soft mechanical bleat. It was the sixth or seventh time in the last week; he'd have to get Cole to fix that, too. The winds sweeping off the plain could be vicious; on a bad day, they rattled the doors to the surface structures hard enough to set off all of the sensors.

Still, good thing I was here... once the Planet was fully staffed, there'd always be someone in control to reset the sensors, but for the time being, he was the only one with access to the control room. If he'd been in bed, the soft but insistent alarm currently going off in his private room would have forced him to get up.

Reston reached for the switch, glancing at the row of monitors to his left more for form's sake than because he expected to see anything—

—and froze, staring at a screen that showed him the entry room nearly a quarter mile above where he sat, in a view from the ceiling cam in the southeast corner. Four, five people, turning on flashlights, all of them dressed in black. The thin beams of light roamed over the dusty consoles, the walls of meteorological equipment—and illuminated the weapons they were holding in flashes of metal. Guns and rifles.

Oh, no.

Reston felt almost a full second of fear and despair before he remembered who he was. Jay Reston had not become one of the most powerful men in the country, perhaps in the world, by panicking.

He reached beneath the console, reached for the slender handset tucked into the slot next to the chair that would connect him directly to White Umbrella's private offices. As soon as he picked it up, the line went through.

"This is Reston," he said, and could hear the steel in his voice, hear it and feel it. "We have a problem. I want a call put in to Trent, I want Jackson to call me immediately—and send out a team, now, I want them here twenty minutes ago."

He stared at the screen as he spoke, at the *intruders*, and clenched his jaw, his initial fear turning to anger. The fugitive S.T.A.R.S., surely...

It didn't matter. Even if they found the entrance, they didn't have the codes—and whoever they were, they would pay for causing him even a second of distress.

Reston slid the phone back into its slot, folded his arms, and watched the strangers move silently across the screen, wondering if they had any idea that they'd be dead within half an hour.

SEVEN

The building was cold and dark, but there was the soft hum of working machinery to break the silence, to listen to over the pounding of her heart. It wasn't too big, maybe thirty feet by twenty, but it was a single room, big enough to feel unsafe, vulnerable. Small lights blinked randomly all around it, like dozens of eyes watching them from the shadows.

Man, I hate this.

Rebecca trailed the tight beam from her flashlight over the west wall of the building, looking for anything out of the ordinary and trying not to feel sick at the same time. In movies, private detectives and cops who had just crashed someone's house were always strolling calmly around, looking for evidence, as if they owned the place; in real life, breaking in somewhere you were absolutely *not* supposed to be was terrifying. She knew they were in the right, that they were the good guys, but still her palms were damp, her heart hammering, and she wished desperately there were a bathroom she could get to. Her bladder had apparently shrunk to the size of a walnut.

*And it'll have to wait, unless I want to go wet the dirt in enemy territory...*Rebecca didn't.

She leaned in to take a closer look at the machine in front of her, a stand-up device the size of a refrigerator and covered with buttons; the label on the front read, "OGO Relay," whatever that was. As far as she could tell, the room was full of big, clunky machines awash in switches; if all of the other buildings were similarly equipped, finding Trent's hidden code panel was going to be an all-night operation.

Each of them had taken a wall, and John was going over the tables in the middle of the room. There was probably a surveillance camera set up somewhere in the building, which made the need to hurry even greater—although they were all hoping that the minimal staff meant no one would be watching. If they were *very* lucky, the security system wouldn't even be hooked up yet.

No, that would be a miracle. Lucky will be if we get in and out of this alive and unhurt, with or without that book...

Since they'd walked away from the van, Rebecca's internal alarms had been ticking down to a full-blown case of the nerves. From her short time with the S.T.A.R.S. she'd learned that trusting her gut feelings was important, maybe even more important than having a weapon; instinct told people to duck bullets, to hide when the enemy was near, to know when to wait and when to act.

The problem is, how do you know if it's instinct or if you're just scared shitless? She didn't know. What she knew was that she wasn't feeling good about their late-night raid; she was cold and jumpy, her stomach hurt, and she couldn't shake the belief that something bad was going to happen.

On the other hand, she *should* be scared—they all should be; what they were doing was dangerous. Something bad might actually happen, acknowledging it wasn't paranoid, it was realistic—

—hello. What's that?

Just to the right of the OGO machine was something that looked like a water heater, a tall, rounded device with a window in the front. Behind the small square of glass was a spool of graph paper, covered with thready black lines, nothing she recognized—what had caught her eye was the dust on the glass. It was the same finely powdered dirt that seemed to be on everything in the room... except it wasn't. There was a smudge across the dirt, a damp streak that may have been caused by someone's finger.

A smudge on dirt?

If someone had run their hand over the dusty glass, they would have cleared a path. Rebecca touched it, frowning—and felt the pebbled surface of the dust, the tiny ridges and whorls like sandpaper beneath her fingers. It was painted or sprayed on—that is, fake.

"Might have something," she whispered, and

touched the window where the smudge was. The window popped open, swinging out—

—and there was a sparkling metal square behind it, a ten-key set into an extremely undusty-looking panel; the graph paper was also fake, just a part of the glass.

"Bingo," John whispered from behind her, and Rebecca stepped back, feeling a flush of excitement as the others gathered around, feeling the tension coming from all of them. The mist of their combined breath made a small cloud in the freezing room, reminding her of how cold she was.

Too cold... we should go back to the van, back to the hotel for a hot bath... She could hear the desperation in her inner voice. It wasn't the cold, it was this place.

"Brilliant," David said softly, and stepped forward, holding his flashlight up. He'd memorized Trent's codes, eleven in all, each eight digits long.

"It'll be the last one, watch," John whispered. Rebecca might have laughed if she wasn't so scared.

John fell silent as they watched him plug in the first numbers, Rebecca thinking that if they didn't work she wouldn't be all that disappointed.

* * *

Jackson had called, informing Reston in his cool, cultured tones that two four-man teams were on their way by helicopter from Salt Lake City. "It so happens that our branch office was entertaining a few of the troops," he'd said. "We have Trent to thank for that; he suggested that we start relocating some of our security in advance of the grand opening, so to speak."

Reston had been glad to hear it, but wasn't so happy about the fact that they were *there*, three armed men and two women poking around the Planet's entrance in the middle of the night—

"They can't get in, Jay," he'd interrupted, gently, soothingly. "They don't have access."

Reston had swallowed his knee-jerk response to that, thanking him instead. Jackson Cortlandt was probably the most patronizing and arrogant son of a bitch Reston had ever known, but he was also extremely competent—and extremely savage if need be; the last man who'd crossed Jackson had been mailed to his family in pieces. Saying "No shit" to the senior member was akin to walking off a tall building.

Jackson had then made it quite clear that while he appreciated the call, it would be best for Jay to handle such matters himself in the future—that if he'd bothered to keep himself apprised of internal shiftings, he would have known about the teams in SLC. There was no explicit wrist-slapping, but Reston got the message all the same; he hung up feeling as though he'd been severely chastised; watching the five interlopers search the entry building only added to his mounting tension.

No codes, no access, even if they find the controls.

Twenty minutes. All he had to do was wait for twenty minutes, half an hour at the outside. Reston took a deep breath, blowing it out slowly—

—and forgot to inhale again as he saw one of them, a girl, push on the window to the keypad. They'd found it, and he still didn't know who they were or how they knew about the Planet—but the way one of the men stepped forward and started punching keys suggested that twenty minutes could be too long to wait for help.

He's guessing, random numbers, it's not possible—

Reston watched the tall, dark-haired man continue to tap in numbers and thought about what Trent had said at their last gathering. That White Umbrella might have a leak.

An information leak, from someone high up. Someone who might know the entry codes.

He reached for the phone again and then stopped, Jackson's subtle warning making him break out in a light sweat. He had to handle it, he had to keep them from getting in, but everyone was asleep and there wasn't an intercom, there was a gun in his room but if they *had* the code, he didn't have time to—

—override.

Reston turned away from the screen and started for the door, kicking himself as he hurried out of control. There was a manual override switch in a hidden panel next to the elevator, he could keep the lift down even if they had the entrance numbers—

—and the teams will come and collect our little pack of invaders, and I will have handled it.

He smiled, a smile entirely without humor, and broke into a run.

* * *

Leon watched anxiously as David typed in another string of numbers, hoping their presence hadn't been detected yet. He hadn't seen a camera, but that didn't mean there wasn't one; if Umbrella could build massive underground laboratories and create monsters, they could hide a video camera.

David hit a final key—and there was sound and movement at once, the low hiss of hidden hydraulics, the distant hum of an engine. A giant piece of the wall to the right of the keypad slid upward. As one, all five of them raised weapons—and lowered them again when they saw the thick mesh gate and the black and empty elevator shaft behind it.

"Damn," John said, a tone of awe in his voice, and Leon had to agree. The panel was ten feet across, thick and heavy with machinery, and had completely disappeared into the ceiling in two seconds. Whatever mechanism was operating it was exceptionally powerful.

"What's that?" Rebecca whispered, and Leon heard it a second later, a distant hum. Apparently the entry code had also recalled the elevator; they could hear it rising, hear the growing echo of well-oiled sound in the freezing darkness of the shaft. It was rising fast, but was still a long way down. Leon wondered, not for the first time, how the hell Umbrella had managed to build such a thing; the Raccoon lab had also been massive, with God-knew-how-many floors of laboratory, all of it deep beneath the surface of the city.

They must have more money than God. And one hell of an architect.

"We may have triggered a warning device or alarm," David said quietly. "It might not be empty."

Leon nodded along with everyone else; they were all silent and tense as they waited, John pointing his rifle at the mesh gate.

* * *

Reston found the flat, seamless panel, and pried it open without any trouble—

—but there was a lock on the switch, a thin metal rod hooked through the top, keeping it from being pushed down. It wasn't until he saw the lock that he recalled it; yet another of Umbrella's precautions, one that suddenly seemed monumentally stupid.

The keys, the workers all have them, I got a set before I came—

Reston ran his hands through his hair, wracking his brain, feeling desperate and harried. *Where'd I put the goddamn security keys?*

When he heard the lift being recalled to the surface only seconds later, it was all he could do to keep from screaming. They had the code. They had guns and there were five of them and they had the code.

Takes two minutes to get to the top, I've still got time and the keys are—

Blank. His mind was blank, and the seconds were ticking past. He'd already hit the recall button, but it wouldn't bring the elevator back down if someone opened the gate on the surface. For all he knew, the assassins or saboteurs or whatever the hell they were had already pried opened the gate, were now watching the lift on its way up, waiting—

—or maybe throwing a few pounds of plastique into the shaft—or—

—control, they're in control!

Reston turned and ran, across the wide corridor and ten feet to the right, down the small offshoot outside of control. His first day at the Planet, one of the construction people had shown him all of the internal locks—backup generator, drug cabinet in surgical... manual override for the lift. He'd yawned his way through that particular tour, then tossed the keys into a drawer in the control room, knowing that he wouldn't be needing them.

He hurried through the door, deciding that he could berate himself for forgetting the keys later, wondering how things had gone so out of control in such a short period of time. Only ten minutes ago he'd been sipping brandy, relaxing—

—and ten minutes from now, you could be dead.

Reston hurried.

* * *

The elevator was big, at least ten feet across and twelve deep. John squinted as it rose into view, the harsh light from a naked bulb in the ceiling nearly blinding after their long stint in darkness.

At least it's empty. Now all we gotta do is avoid getting ambushed and murdered when we hit the bottom.

The elevator came to a smooth stop. The latch on the mesh gate unlocked and the gate slid into the wall. John was closest. He glanced at David, who nodded a go-ahead.

"First floor, shoes, menswear, Umbrella assholes," John said, not particularly bothered that he didn't get a laugh. Everyone had their own preferred method for dealing with tension. Besides, his sense of humor was more fully developed.

Right over their heads, he thought, scanning the walls of the elevator car for anything unusual. Well, maybe not over their heads; it was more that they just didn't appreciate his fine wit. He kept himself amused, that was the important thing, it kept him from freezing up or turning into a basket case.

The elevator looked okay, dusty but solid. John stepped carefully inside, Leon right behind—

—then John heard a noise, just as a red light started to blink on the lift's control panel.

"Be still," John hissed, holding his hand up, not wanting anyone else to get on until he saw what the light was for—

—and the mesh gate closed behind him, the latch snapping shut. He spun, saw that Leon was on board, saw Claire and Rebecca lunging for the gate from the other side and David running for the keypad.

There was a rasping *click* from overhead and Leon, closer to the front, shouted at Claire and Rebecca—

"Get back!"

—because the wall panel was coming down, *slamming* down, and the girls were stumbling back. John caught a final glimpse of their shocked and pale faces in the gloom—

—and the door had closed, and although he hadn't touched a thing, the elevator was going down. John crouched by the controls, punching at the buttons, and saw what the flashing red light was for.

"Manual override," he said, and stood up, looking at the young cop, not sure what to say. Their simple plan had just been totally screwed.

"Shit," Leon said, and John nodded, thinking he'd summed it up perfectly.

EIGHT

"Shit," Claire hissed, feeling helpless and afraid, wanting to beat against the wall panel until it released the two men.

Trap, it was a trap, a setup—

"Listen... it's going down," Rebecca said, and Claire heard it, too. She turned, saw David tapping the keypad with one hand, flashlight in the other, his face grim.

"David," Claire started, and stopped as David spared her a pointed glance, a look that told her to wait. He barely paused in his number punching, returning his entire attention back to the controls.

She turned to Rebecca, saw that Rebecca was chewing at her lip nervously, watching David.

"He must be trying all the codes," she whispered to Claire, and Claire nodded, feeling sick with worry, wanting to talk action but realizing that David needed to concentrate. She compromised, leaning in to whisper back to Rebecca; if she just stood there quietly in the freezing dark, she'd lose her mind.

"Think it was Trent?"

Rebecca frowned, then shook her head. "No. I think we hit a silent alarm or something. I saw a light flashing in the elevator before the gate closed."

Rebecca sounded just as scared as she was, just as *terrified*, and Claire thought about how close she and John must have gotten. As close as Leon and herself, maybe. Claire instinctively reached for her hand and Rebecca took it, squeezing it tightly, both of them watching David.

Come on, one of them has to open it, to bring it back...

A few tense seconds passed, and David stopped hitting keys. He pointed the flashlight up, the reflection just enough light to see each other by.

"Seems that the numbers don't work if the lift is in use," he said. His voice was calm and easy, but Claire could see that his jaw was clenched, the muscles in his cheeks twitching.

"I'll try them all again in a moment, and then again—but since someone else seems to have access to the lift's master control, we should start considering other options. Rebecca—start looking for a camera, check the corners and ceiling; if we're going to be here awhile, we'll need privacy. Claire, see if you can find any tools we might use to get through the wall—tire iron, screwdriver, anything. If the codes won't work, we'll see if we can't force our way in. Questions?"

"No," Rebecca said, and Claire shook her head.

"Good. Take a deep breath and get to it."

David went back to the keypad and Rebecca walked to the corner, turning her flashlight to the ceiling. Claire took a deep breath and turned, looking at the dusty table in the middle of the room. It had stacked drawers on either side; she opened the first, pushing aside papers and clutter, thinking that David really kicked ass under pressure.

Tire iron, screwdriver, anything... be careful, please be careful and don't get killed...

Claire forced herself to take another deep breath; then she opened the next drawer, continuing her search.

* * *

John took the lead, which Leon was only too happy to follow. He may have survived Raccoon, but the ex-S.T.A.R.S. soldier had been in and out of combat situations for something like nine years; he won.

"Get down," John said, crouching himself, then lying down on his stomach and wrapping the M-16 strap tightly around his muscular arm. "If it's an ambush, they'll be aiming high when the door opens; we take out their knees. Works like a charm."

Leon lay down next to him, propping his right arm up with his left hand, his nine-millimeter pointed loosely at the gate. Outside, the darkness slid past, nothing to see but metal-lined shaft. "And if it's not?"

"Stand up, you take the right, I'll take left, stay in

the car if you can. If you find yourself aiming at a wall, turn around and shoot low."

John glanced over at him—incredibly, a wide grin was spreading across his face. "Think of all the fun they're going to miss. We get to blow some Umbrella guys all to shit, and they're stuck in the cold dark with nothing to do."

Leon was a little too tense to smile back, although he made an effort. "Yeah, some guys get all the luck," he said.

John shook his head, his grin fading. "Nothing we can do but go for the ride," he said, and Leon nodded, swallowing. John might be crazy, but he was right about that much. They were where they were, wishing otherwise wouldn't make it so.

Doesn't hurt to try, though. Christ, I wish we hadn't stepped on this thing...

The elevator kept going down, and they both fell silent, waiting. Leon was glad that John wasn't the chatty type; he liked to crack jokes, but it was obvious that he didn't take a dangerous situation lightly. Leon saw that he was breathing deeply, sighting the M-16, preparing for whatever was going to happen.

Leon took a few deep breaths himself, trying to relax into the prone position—

—and the elevator stopped. There was a soft ping sound, a chime, and the mesh gate was moving, disappearing into its designated hole in the wall. A windowless outer door rose at the same time, mellow light spilled across them—

—and there was nobody. A polished concrete wall twenty feet away, a polished concrete floor. Gray emptiness.

Get up, go!

Leon scrambled to his feet, heart beating too fast, John silent and even faster to his left. An exchanged glance and they both took one step out of the elevator, Leon whipping his VP70 around right, ready to fire—

—and there was nothing. Again. A wide corridor that seemed a mile long, the faint, mingled scents of dust and some industrial disinfectant in the cool air. Cool, but not at all cold; compared to the surface, it was summer. The hall was a hundred and fifty yards easy, maybe more; there were a few offshoots, rounded lights spaced at regular intervals along the ceiling, no signs posted—and no sign of life either.

So who brought us down? And why, if they weren't planning on meeting us with a few bullets?

"Maybe they're all playing bingo," John said softly, and Leon looked back, saw that except for the placement of a few side halls, John's side was identical to his. And just as empty.

They both stepped back into the elevator. John reached for the controls, tapped the "Up" button, and nothing happened.

"What now?" Leon asked.

"Don't ask me, David's the brains behind our outfit," John said. "Though I got the looks."

"Jesus, John," Leon said, frustrated. "You've got seniority here; give me a break, will ya?"

John shrugged. "Okay. Here's what I'm thinking. Maybe it wasn't a trap. Maybe... if it *was* a trap, they would've tried to get all of us. And we'd be in the middle of a firefight right now."

And the timing. The elevator was only there for a few seconds—as if someone realized we'd called it up...

"Someone was trying to keep us from getting on, weren't they?" Leon said, not really asking. "To keep us from coming down."

John nodded. "Give that man a cigar. And if that's right, it means they're scared of us. I mean, there's no security, right? Whoever brought us down probably hightailed it to a room with a lock.

"As to what we do now," he continued, "I'm open to suggestions. It'd be nice to rejoin our group, but if we can't figure out how to get the elevator going..."

Leon frowned, thinking, remembering that before Raccoon had pretty much blown his career choice, he *had* been trained as a cop.

Use the tools you've got...

"Secure the area," he said slowly. "Same plan as before, at least the first part. Get the employees secured, then worry about the elevator. Dealing with Reston will just have to wait—"

John held up his hand suddenly, cutting him off, his head cocked to one side. Leon listened, but didn't hear anything. A few seconds passed and then John lowered his hand. He shrugged dismissively, but his dark eyes were wary and he held the automatic rifle close.

"Good call," he said finally. "If we can *find* the damn employees. You wanna go left or right?"

Leon smiled faintly, suddenly remembering the last time he'd had to pick a direction. He'd taken a left in the sub-basement of Umbrella's Raccoon lab and run into a dead end; having to backtrack had almost cost him his life.

"Right," he said. "Left has some bad associations for me."

John cocked an eyebrow, but didn't say anything; oddly enough, he seemed satisfied with Leon's reasoning.

Maybe because he's crazy. Crazy enough to make bad jokes in the midst of situations like this, anyway.

Together, they stepped out into the long, empty corridor and turned right, moving slowly, John watching their back and Leon scanning every offshoot's opening for a sign of movement. The first side hall was to their left, not fifteen feet from the elevator.

"Hang on," John said, and ducked into the short hall, walking quickly to a single door at the back. He rattled the handle, then hurried back out, shaking his head.

"Thought I heard something before," he said, and Leon nodded, thinking about how easy it would be for someone to kill them.

Hide in a locked room, wait 'til we're past, step out and pow...

Bad thinking. Leon let it go and they continued

their slow trek down the passage, sweeping every inch with their weapons, Leon realizing that the thermal underwear'd been a bad idea, as sweat started to trickle down his body—and wondering, quite abruptly, how things had gone so wrong so fast.

* * *

Reston had an idea.

He'd almost panicked after he'd heard them saying things that they shouldn't have known, hiding in control with the door cracked open. When he'd heard one of them say his name, he'd felt the panic rise into his throat like bile, coloring his mind with visions of his own horrible death. He'd closed the door then, locking it, sagging against it as he tried to think, to sort through his options.

When one of them had rattled the door, he'd very nearly screamed—but had managed to hold still, to make no sound at all until the interloper had moved on. It took him a few moments to collect himself after that, to remember that this was something he could handle; strangely enough, it was the thought of Trent that did it for him. Trent wouldn't panic. Trent would know exactly what to do—and he most certainly wouldn't run crying to Jackson for help.

In spite of that, he'd almost picked up the phone several times as he watched the monitors, watched the two men terrorizing his employees. They were efficient, unlike their fumbling counterparts still working to figure out the elevator on the surface. It had taken the two men all of five minutes once they'd reached the living area to get the workers together; it helped that five of them were still awake and playing cards in the cafeteria, three of the construction crew and both mechanics. The young white man watched them as the other one went to the dorm and roused the rest, marching them back to the cafeteria, crowding them with his automatic weapon.

Reston was disappointed with the lackluster performance of his people, not one fighter among them, and was still very afraid. Once the teams from the city came in he'd have something to work with, but until then, all sorts of bad things might happen.

"Dealing with Reston will just have to wait..." What happens when they realize I'm not in their hostage group? What do they want? What could they want, except to hold me for ransom or kill me?

He'd been on the verge of calling Sidney, in spite of the fact that Jackson would certainly find out about it—but he'd risk his colleague's disapproval, he'd risk losing his place in the inner circle if it meant he could survive this invasion.

He was actually reaching for the phone when he realized that someone was missing. Reston leaned closer to the cafeteria monitor, frowning, forgetting the phone. There were fourteen people grouped together in the middle of the room, the two gunmen standing some distance away.

Where's the other one? Who's the other one?

Reston reached out and touched the screen, marking off the faces of the bleary-eyed hostages. The five construction workers. Two mechanics. The cook, the specimen handlers, all six of them....

"Cole," he muttered, pursing his lips. The electrician, Henry Cole. He wasn't there.

An idea began to form, but it depended on where Cole actually was. Reston tapped at the buttons that worked the screens, beginning to hope, to see a way not only to survive, but to, to—*win.* To come out on top.

There were twenty-two screens in the control room, but almost fifty cameras set up throughout the Planet and in the surface "weather" station. The Planet had been built with video in mind, the layout fairly simple; from control, one could see almost every part of every hall, room, and environment, the cameras placed at key points. Finding someone was just a matter of pushing the right button to switch between views.

Reston checked the test rooms first, each set of cameras in phases One through Four. No luck. He tried the science area next, the surgical rooms, the chem lab, even the stasis room; again, he didn't see anyone.

He wouldn't be in quarters, they've certainly cleared everyone else out... and there's no reason for him to be on the surface...

Reston grinned suddenly, punching up the cameras in and around the holding cells. Cole and both of the mechanics had been using the cells to lay out equipment, wires and tools and various bits of machinery.

There!

Cole was sitting on the floor in between cells one and nine, sorting through a box of little metal pieces, his skinny legs splayed out in front of him.

Reston looked back at the cafeteria, saw that the two armed men seemed to be conferring, watching the useless, huddled group of workers. On the surface, the other three were still hammering at the keypad and searching for something or other...

The idea took shape, the possibilities coming to him one at a time, each more interesting and exciting than the last. The data he could collect, the respect that he would earn, getting rid of his problem and promoting himself at the same time.

I could edit the tapes together, have something to show my visitors after the tour—and won't Sidney be undone when Jackson sees what I've accomplished, how I've handled things. I'll be the golden child for a change...

Reston stood up from the console, still grinning, nervous but hopeful. He'd have to hurry, and he'd have to use all his acting skills with Cole; not a problem, considering that he'd spent thirty years of his life developing them, honing them...Before joining Umbrella, he'd been a diplomat.

It would work. They wanted Reston; he'd give him to them.

NINE

Cole was poking idly through a box of bipolar transistors, thinking that he was an idiot; he should be sleeping. It had to be close to midnight, he'd been breaking his ass all day for Mr. Blue, and he'd have to drag said ass out of bed in another six hours to do the same. He was tired and sick to death of being picked on just because the last happy asshole to go through the Planet with a toolbox had done everything wrong.

It's not my *fault,* he thought sullenly, *that the dumbass didn't connect the leads on the MOSFETs before he installed 'em.* And *his outdoor conduits are crappy, he didn't figure on the Planet's inductive load... incompetent jerkoff...*

Maybe he was being harsh, but he wasn't feeling particularly forgiving after the day he'd had. Mr. Blue had distinctly told him to get to the surface cams first—and then chased him down and *insisted* he'd told him to take care of the intercom system first.

Cole knew he was full of shit—along with everyone else working at the Planet—but Reston was one of the top guys, a real heavy-hitter; when he said jump, you jumped, and there was never a question of who was right. Cole had only worked for Umbrella for a year, but he'd made more money in that year than he had in the five before combined; he was *not* gonna be the one to piss off Mr. Blue (so-called because of his perpetual blue suit) and get himself canned.

You sure about that? After all you've seen in the last few weeks?

Cole put the box of transistors down and rubbed at his eyes; they felt hot and itchy. He hadn't been sleeping all that well since coming to work at the Planet. It wasn't that he was some bleeding-heart type, he didn't give much of a shit what Umbrella wanted to do with their money. But—

—but it's hard to feel good about this place. It's bad news. It's a freak show.

In his year with Umbrella, he'd wired a chem lab on the west coast for power, installed a bunch of new circuit breakers for a think tank on the other coast, and generally done a lot of maintenance work wherever they shipped him. Incredible pay, not too hard, and the people he usually worked with were decent enough—mostly blue-collar types doing the same kind of stuff he was doing. And all he had to do—outside of the work—was promise not to talk about whatever he saw; he'd signed a contract to that effect when he'd first hired on, and had never had a problem with it. But then, he'd never seen the Planet.

When Umbrella called you out on a job, they didn't explain anything. It was just, "fix that," and you fixed it and got paid. Even within the working crews, discussions about the job site's purpose were heavily discouraged. Word got around, though, and Cole knew enough about the Planet to think that he maybe didn't want to work for Umbrella anymore.

There were the creatures, for one thing, the test animals. He hadn't actually seen them, or the thing they were calling Fossil, the frozen freak—but he'd heard them, a couple of times. Once, in the middle of the night, a screeching, howling sound that had chilled him to the bone, a sound like a bird, screaming. And then there was the day in Phase Two, realigning one of the video cameras, when he'd heard a strange chattering sound, like nails being tapped on hollow wood—but the sound was animal, too. Alive. He'd heard that they were specially created for Umbrella, some kind of genetic hybrids that would be better for studying, but hybrids of what? All of the creatures had bizarre and unpleasant nicknames, too. He'd heard the "research" guys talking about them on more than one occasion.

Dacs. Scorps. Spitters. Hunters. Sound like a fun bunch—for a horror movie.

Cole crawled to his feet, stretching his tired muscles, still thinking unhappy thoughts. There was Reston, of course; the guy was a grade-A tyrant, and of the worst kind—the kind with a lot of power and not a lot of patience. Cole was used to working with managerial types, but Mr. Blue was way too high on the food chain for his comfort zone. The man was intimidating as all hell.

But that's not the worst, is it?

He sighed, looking around at the dozen cells that lined the room, six on either side. No, the worst was right in front of him. Each cell had a cot, a toilet, a sink—and restraining straps on the walls and attached to the beds. And the cell block was less than twenty feet from the "foyer" of the first environment, where the doors had locks on the outside.

After this one, I do some serious thinking about my priorities; I've got enough saved to take a break, get some perspective...

Cole sighed again. That was fine, for later. For now, though, he had to try and catch some sleep. He turned and walked to the door, slapping the lights off as he opened it—

—and there was Reston. Hurrying around the corner where the main corridor turned toward the elevators, looking extremely upset.

Oh, hell, what now?

Reston saw him and practically *ran* to him, his blue suit uncharacteristically rumpled, his pale gaze darting left and right.

"Henry," he gasped, and stopped in front of him, breathing hard. "Thank God. You have to help me. There are two men, assassins, they broke in and they're here to kill me, and I need your help."

Cole was as much taken aback by his demeanor as by what he said; he'd never seen Blue with a hair out of place, or without that small, smug smile that was the sole property of the incredibly wealthy.

"I—what?"

Reston took a deep breath, blowing it out slowly. "I'm sorry. I just—the Planet has been invaded; there are two men here, looking for *me*. They mean to kill me, Henry. I recognize them from a thwarted attempt on my life not six months ago; they've posted a man on the surface by the door, and I'm trapped, they'll find me and—"

He broke off, gasping, and was he trying not to *cry*? Cole stared at him, thinking *he called me Henry*. "Why are they trying to kill you?" he asked.

"I was the chair for a hostile takeover last year, a packaging company—the man we bought out was unstable, he swore he'd get me. And now they're here, right now they're locking up everyone in the cafeteria—but they're only after me—I've called for help but they won't get here in time. Please, Henry— will you help me? I—I'll make it worth your while, I promise you. You'll never have to work again, your *children* will never have to work..."

The open plea in Reston's eyes was disconcerting; it stopped Cole from mentioning that he didn't have any children. The man was terrified, his lined face quivering, his silver-shot hair sticking up in tufts. Even without the monetary offer, Cole would have offered to help.

Maybe.

"What do you want me to do?"

Reston half-smiled in relief, actually reaching out to grasp Cole's arm. "Thank you, Henry. Thank you, I—I'm not sure. If you could—they only want me, so if you could distract them somehow..."

He frowned, his lips trembling, then looked past Cole to the small room that marked the entrance to the environments. "That room! It has a lock on the outside, and opens into One—if you could lure them to you, slip into One... I could lock them inside, lock down the entire room as soon as you were out. You could go straight through to Four and out to the medical area, I'd unlock it for you as soon as they're trapped."

Cole nodded uncertainly. It should work, except—

"Won't they know I'm not you? I mean, they'll have a picture of you or something, won't they?"

"They won't be able to tell. They'll only see you for a second, when they come around the corner, and then you'll be gone. As soon as they get inside, I'll hit the controls—I can hide in the cell block."

Reston's pale eyes were swimming, overbright with unshed tears. The guy was desperate—and as plans went, it wasn't a bad one.

"Yeah, okay," he said, and the look of gratitude on the older man's face was almost heartwarming.

Almost. If he were a decent human being it would be.

"You won't regret this, Henry," Reston said, and

Cole nodded, not sure what else to say.

"You'll be fine, Mr. Reston," he said finally, uncomfortably. "Don't worry."

"I'm sure you're right, Henry," Reston said, and turned, and walked into the dark cell block without another word.

Cole stood there for a second, then shrugged inwardly and started for the little room, nervous but also a little peeved. Mr. Blue was scared, but he was still pretty much an asshole.

No "Don't you worry either, Henry," or, "Be careful." Not even a "Good luck, hope they don't shoot you by mistake."...

He shook his head, stepping into the small room. At least if he helped out the big Blue he'd probably be able to sleep in, maybe even quit the Planet and Umbrella for good. God knew he needed the rest; he'd been having a hell of a time sleeping...

* * *

Rebecca found the camera, at least. A lens no bigger than a quarter was hidden in the southwest corner, just an inch from the ceiling. She'd called David over and he'd covered it with his hand, wishing that he'd done a more thorough check before leading his team inside. He'd been stupid, and John and Leon were almost certainly gone because of it.

Claire had found a roll of tape in her diggings, though little else. David taped the hole over, wondering what they were going to do. It was cold, so cold that he didn't know how much longer their reflexes would still be good. The codes weren't working, the sealed entrance would take more than they had to open it up, and two of his team were somewhere in the facility below, perhaps wounded, perhaps dying...

...or infected. Infected like Steve and Karen were infected, suffering, losing their humanity—

"Stop it," Rebecca said to him, and he stepped down from the table they'd pushed to the corner, half knowing what she meant but not ready to admit it. Rebecca had a way of drawing him out at the worst possible times.

"Stop what?"

Rebecca stepped closer to him, staring up into his face, hooding her flashlight with one small hand.

"You know what. You've got that look, I can see it; you're telling yourself that this is your fault. That if you'd done something differently, they'd still be here."

He sighed. "I appreciate your concern, but this isn't the appropriate—"

"Yes it is," she interrupted. "If you're going to blame yourself, you won't think as clearly. We're not in the S.T.A.R.S. anymore, and you're not anyone's captain. It's not your fault."

Claire had walked over to join them, her gray gaze curious and searching in spite of the worry that still pinched her delicate features. "You think this is your fault? It's not. I don't think that."

David threw up his hands. "My God, alright! It's not

my fault, and we can all spend some time analyzing what I'm accountable for if and when we get out of this; for now, though, can we please concentrate on what's in front of us?"

Both young women nodded, and while he was glad to have stopped the therapy session before it got started, he realized that he didn't know what the next thing was—what tasks to give them beyond what they'd already done, how they were going to resolve their crisis, what to say or how to say it. It was a dreadful moment; he was used to having something to fight against, something to react to or shoot at or plan for, but their situation seemed to be static, unchanging. There wasn't a clear path for them to follow, and that was even worse than the guilt he felt about his lack of foresight.

And just at that moment, he heard the distant buzz of an approaching helicopter, the faraway *thrum* that could be nothing else—and although it was a solution of sorts, it was the worst one possible.

Nothing for cover except this compound, and we'll never make it back to the van, we've got two, three minutes—

"We have to get out of here," David said, already running through the things they would have to do if they were to stand a chance, even as they were all running for the door.

* * *

The workers were cake. There had been a few tense moments rousing them from their dark cots in the dark dorm rooms, but it had gone off without incident. John had still been somewhat wary of a few of them when he'd first herded them into the cafeteria, where Leon was watching the card-players—in particular, two fairly big men who looked like they might have machismo disorders and a thin, twitchy guy with deepset eyes who couldn't seem to stop licking his lips. It was like a compulsive thing; every few seconds, his tongue would dart out, flick between his lips and then disappear for another few seconds. Creepy.

There'd been no trouble, though. Fourteen men and no one willing to play hero after John had presented them with a little logic. He'd kept it short and simple: we're here to find something, we're not planning to hurt anyone, we just want you to stay out of the way while we get out of here. Don't be stupid and you won't get shot. Either the logic or the M-16 had been enough to convince them that it would be best not to argue.

John stood by the door back into the big hall, watching the unhappy-looking group seated in the middle of the large room around a long table. A few looked pissed, a few looked scared, most just looked tired. Nobody spoke, which was fine by John; he didn't want to have to worry about anyone trying to work up a rebellion.

In spite of his reasonable certainty that all was cool, he was glad to hear the light tap on the door. Leon had been gone maybe five minutes, but it seemed like a lot longer. He walked in holding a length of chain and a couple of wire coat hangers.

"Any trouble?" Leon asked quietly, and John shook his head, keeping his attention on the silent group.

"Been nice and quiet," he said. "Where'd you find the chain?"

"Toolbox, in one of the rooms."

John nodded, then raised his voice, keeping it calm. "Alright, folks, we're about to take our leave. We thank you for your patience..."

Leon nudged him. "Ask if Reston's here," he whispered.

John sighed. "You think if he is, he's gonna tell *us*?"

The younger man shrugged. "Worth a shot, isn't it?"

Stranger things have happened...

John cleared his throat and spoke again. "Is a man named Reston in here? We just have a question, we're not going to hurt you."

The men stared at him, at both of them, and John wondered, for just a second, if they knew what they were doing there; if they knew what Umbrella was doing. They didn't *look* like Nazis, they looked like a bunch of working stiffs. Like guys who put in a hard day and liked to throw back a few beers in the evening. Like—like guys.

And what did Nazis look like? These people are a part of the problem, they're working for the enemy. They're not going to help us—

"Blue ain't here." A big bearded man in a T-shirt and boxers, one of the ones John had been keeping an eye on. His voice was gruff and irritable, his face still puffy from sleep.

John glanced at Leon, surprised, and saw that the rookie looked the same. "Blue?" John asked. "Is that Reston?"

A man sitting at the end of the table with longish hair and grease-stained hands nodded. "Yeah. And that's *Mister* Blue to you."

The sarcasm was pointed. There were a couple of dark looks exchanged within the sitting group—and a couple of chuckles.

Reston's one of the key guys, Trent said. And just about everybody hates their boss... but so much that they'd talk shit about him to a couple of terrorists?

Reston must be *real* unpopular.

"Is there anyone else working here who isn't in this room?" Leon asked. "We don't want to be surprised..."

The implications were obvious, but it was also obvious that they weren't going to get anything else from the assembled employees. They might hate Reston, but John could see from the crossed arms and scowls that they wouldn't talk about one of their own. *If* there was anyone else in the facility, which he doubted. Trent had said it was a small staff...

...which means it was probably Reston who brought us down, which means we could kill two birds if we find him—get the book and get him to start up the elevator again. We lock Reston in a closet, hook up with David and the girls and get gone before anything else unexpected comes up.

John nodded at Leon, and they backed up to the door. John realized that he didn't want to just walk out, that he felt a kind of sympathy for the men that he'd dragged out of bed. Not a lot, but something.

"We're gonna lock the door here," John said, "but you'll be okay until the company sends someone, you got food... and if you don't mind a little advice, listen up—Umbrella ain't the good guys. Whatever they're paying you, it isn't enough. They're killers."

The blank stares followed them out of the room. Leon closed the double doors and started to rig up the makeshift lock, threading the chain through the handles and bending the hangers. John walked the few steps to the corner and looked down the long gray hall that they'd stepped into from the elevator. They could continue on the way they'd been going to look for Reston, there was a bend in the corridor not far past the staff housing area—

—*but he's not that way*, John thought, remembering the sound he'd heard when they'd first arrived. *He's back the way we came, somewhere.*

Leon finished securing the doors and joined him, looking a little pale but still game. "So... now we look for Reston?"

"Yeah," John said, thinking that the kid was doing pretty well, considering. Not a lot of experience, but he was smart, he had guts, and he didn't clutch under the gun. "You holding up?"

Leon nodded. "Yeah. I'm just—do you think they're okay up there?"

"No, I think they're freezing their asses off waiting for us," John said, smiling, and hoped that was the case—that after locking down the elevator, Reston hadn't released the hounds, or whatever equivalent this place had.

Or called for help...

"Let's get this over with," John said, and Leon nodded, as they started back down the hall to see what was what.

TEN

They headed out into the blackness of the compound, the beat of the helicopter's blades getting closer. Rebecca saw its lights less than a half-mile northwest, saw that it was hovering, shining a spotlight down onto the desert-like plain.

The van, they've spotted the van.

Claire saw it too, but David was looking at the warehouse-type buildings behind them as he unslung his rifle, his intense gaze taking in the layout. Rebecca could hardly see him in the pale moonlight.

"They'll have to set down outside the fence," he said. "Follow me, and stay close." He jogged off into the darkness, the burr of the helicopter growing steadily behind them.

God, I hope he sees better than I can, Rebecca thought, clutching her nine-millimeter tightly, the metal cold against her numb fingers. She and Claire jogged after him as he headed for one of the dark structures, the second from the left in the line of five. Why he'd picked that one she didn't know, but David would have a reason, he always did.

They ran into the corridor of black between the first and second building, fifteen feet of hard-packed arid sediment that stretched ahead of them some indeterminate distance. The freezing air burned into her lungs, gusting out in clouds of steam she couldn't see. The *whackawhacka* sound of the 'copter drowned out their footsteps, drowned out most of what David was saying as he stopped, a door on either side of them.

"... to hide until we... can't... back..."

Rebecca shook her head and David gave it up, turning to the left, pointing his weapon at the door of the first building. Rebecca and Claire moved behind him, Rebecca wondering what he was up to; if the people from the helicopter landed to search—which they surely would—the bullet-riddled door would give them away. It looked to be made from some high-density plastic, but wasn't remarkable in any other way—it had a handle and keyhole rather than a card swipe. The building itself was some kind of stucco material, dirty and dusty, and no particular color that she could tell; the one behind them looked the same; there were no windows on either.

The helicopter's searchlight was sweeping the fence at the front of the compound, its brightness piercing the cold dark like a brilliant flame. Flurries of dust were swirling up into the light, staining it, and Rebecca thought they had maybe a minute before it found them; the compound just wasn't that big.

Bambambambambam!

Most of the noise was swallowed up by the roar of the helicopter. Even in the darkness, Rebecca could see the line of holes, the concentration of them near the handle. David stepped forward and gave the door a hard kick, then a second—and it flew inward, a gaping black hole in the wall.

The searchlight was moving back through the compound, the helicopter's swollen belly passing almost directly overhead as it shone its beam down on the other side of the first building, the thunder of its engine and billowing clouds of dust making Rebecca feel as though Death were approaching; not death but Death, some fabled beast of merciless power and relentless intention...

David turned and grabbed her and Claire both, pushing them firmly toward the open door. As soon as they were through, he motioned for them to stop and to wait. David pulled his handgun and jogged across the open space, standing close to the second building's door, angling his body and—

—*BAM*, the nine-millimeter round, louder than the rifle's .223s but still almost lost, as the helicopter started its sweep up *their* row and the door blasted inward and David leapt through the opening, just as the blinding light illuminated the ground between them. A half-second later and he would have been caught in the light. The spent casings from David's weapons were thankfully lost in the furor, spinning clouds of dust whipping up and over them and making it hard to breathe. She turned, saw that Claire had tucked her face down into her black sweatshirt, and followed suit. The cold, thick air was filtered through the fleece, and in spite of the deafening noise, Rebecca could hear her heartbeat in her ears, rapid and afraid.

A second later, the light was past; a second after that the dust seemed to be settling, it was hard to tell in the black; the sudden absence of light meant their eyes would have to readjust—

"*Are you alright?*"

Rebecca jumped as David practically screamed in her face, just a shadow in front of her. Claire let out a little shriek.

"Sorry!" David called. "Come on! Other building!"

Barely able to see, Rebecca stumbled outside, Claire right next to her. David came up behind them, touching their backs, guiding them toward the second building. The 'copter was still moving away from them, north to south, but it would run out of things to look at very soon—and then they'd land and come looking. That the helicopter was from Umbrella was a given; the only question was how many had come, and whether or not they were to be captured first or just killed outright.

As they fell through the door to the second building, it dawned on Rebecca what David had done. The Umbrella thugs would see the first bullet-blasted door and assume that their quarry was hiding there.

And he only shot through the keyhole of this one.

They'll see it eventually, but it buys us a little more time...

She hoped. The darkness was almost as cold as outside and smelled like dust. A low light flickered on, David hooding his flashlight with one hand, just enough for them to see that they were surrounded by boxes. Big ones, small ones, cardboard and wood, stacked on shelves and on the floor all the way up to the slanted ceiling. In the brief second that David shone the light across the mammoth room, they saw that there had to be thousands of them.

"I'm going to see what I can do about the door and cut the lights," David said. "Find us a place to hide. It's our best option until we know how many there are, what scenario they're employing. They might have spook eyes, the floor's no good—somewhere high up and in a corner. Shelves would be best. Got it?"

They both nodded and the light went out, leaving them in a complete darkness; before, she could at least make out shapes and shadows. Now, Rebecca couldn't see her hand in front of her face.

"Which corner?" Claire whispered, as if the chill black nothing they stood in demanded silence.

Rebecca reached out and found Claire's hand, placing it against her back. "Left. We go left until we run into something."

She heard a whisper of movement behind them, as David went about his preparations. Taking a deep breath, Rebecca put her hands out in front of her and started to edge forward.

* * *

Every door off of the lengthy corridor was locked, with the exception of a utility closet past the elevator; there, they found absolutely nothing of interest, unless shelves of paper towels and styrene coffee cups were interesting. They'd tried the elevator again, with no luck, and there didn't seem to be a fuse box or override switch anywhere near it. Not surprising, but Leon still felt a pang of distress. The other three were probably really worried...

...and you're not? What if something went wrong up there? Maybe the "test" part of this place is above-ground. And maybe Reston unleashed some of Umbrella's warrior specimens up there, and right now Claire is—

"What say if we run across one more locked door, we use up our grenades? I've got two of 'em," John said, looking irritated. They'd just tried the ninth door in the silent hall, and were almost to the northernmost curve. For all they knew, they'd already passed Reston, or the passage that would lead them to him.

"Let's at least see what's around the corner before we start blowing things up," Leon said, though he was also losing patience. It wasn't that he'd mind damaging some Umbrella property, but that just wasn't the priority—reuniting the team was. They'd already decided that if they didn't find him soon, they'd go back to the cafeteria and try to get one of the workers to fix the elevator, and to hell with Reston; the mission would be a bust, but at least they'd all be alive to fight another day.

Assuming we're all still alive now...

They reached the corner and paused, John raising the M-16 and lowering his voice. "I'll cover?"

Leon nodded, moving closer to the inner wall. "On three. One... two... *three*—"

He took a running step away from the wall, dropping into a crouch and pointing his semi down the west leg of the corridor as John whipped the rifle around the corner. The hall was a lot shorter, no more than sixty feet, dead-ending in an open, doorless room. There was a door on the left—

—and somebody moved across the opening at the end of the hall, the darting shape of a man.

Reston.

Leon saw him, a thin guy, not too tall, wearing jeans and a blue work shirt. Mr. Blue, just like they said...

"Hold it!" John shouted, and Reston turned, startled—and weaponless. He saw the M-16 and jumped away from the double-wide opening, maybe heading for an exit—

—and Leon ran, pumping his arms for speed, John quickly passing him in a full-on sprint. They were inside the room in a flash and there was Reston, pushing desperately at a door on the right. He threw a terrified glance over his shoulder as they barreled into the room, his eyes wide with panic.

"It won't open!" He screamed, his voice on the edge of hysteria. "*Open the door!*"

Who's he talking to?

"Give it up, Reston," John growled—

—and behind them, a metal sheet crashed down over the opening, shutting them into the room with a brutal, heavy *clang*. Leon looked down, saw that the floor was plate steel—and felt the first stab of unease.

Reston spun around, his hands in the air, his narrow features contorted with fear. "I'm not him, not Reston," he babbled, his pale face slick with sweat—

—and behind them, a face appeared at the window in the metal door, distorted by the thick plexiglass but obviously grinning. An older man, dressed in a dark blue suit.

Oh, no—

The man looked away for a moment, one hand reaching up to touch something Leon couldn't see— and a smooth, cultured voice floated into the room from a speaker in the ceiling.

"Sorry, Henry," the man said, his moving face warped by the glass. "And allow me to introduce myself. I'm Jay Reston. And whoever you are, I'm *very* glad to meet you. Welcome to the Planet's test program."

Leon looked at John, who was still pointing his rifle at the near hysterical Henry. John looked back at him, and Leon could see the awareness dawning in his dark eyes, even as it dawned on him.

They were in extremely deep shit.

* * *

Yes!

Reston laughed giddily. The gunmen were trapped, and the three on the surface were probably already being picked up by the teams—he'd handled his situation, and handled it brilliantly.

Of course it's no fun if there's no one around to appreciate it... but then, I have a captive audience, don't I?

"We're not scheduled to go on line for another twenty-three days," Reston said, smiling widely, already imagining the look on Sidney's bloated face. "At which time, I was going to host the initial run of our carefully designed program for a group of extremely important people. It was going to be spedmen only, we hadn't planned on putting humans through the phases for a while yet, let alone *soldiers.* But now, thanks to you, I'll be able to show my little party actual footage of what our specimens were created for. By now, your friends on the surface will have been taken, sad to say—but the three of you will suffice, I think. Yes, you'll do quite nicely."

Reston laughed again, unable to contain it. "You may want to kill Henry before you start, though, he'll only drag you down—and he *did* lure you in, didn't he?"

"*You bastard!*"

Henry Cole pushed away from the wall and flew at the door, pounding on it with his fists. The two-inch metal didn't even rattle in the frame.

Reston shook his head, still grinning. "I *am* sorry, Henry; we'll miss you terribly. You never did finish with the intercom system, did you? Or the audio... at least you hooked up *this* one, for which I can't thank you enough. Is it clear enough in there? Getting any static?"

Whatever demon had possessed the electrician fled, the man collapsing against the door, breathing raggedly. The bigger of the two armed men, the burly dark-skinned one with the rifle, stepped toward the window with a menacing expression.

"You're not gonna get us to go through any tests for you," he said, his deep voice quivering with rage. "Go ahead and kill us, 'cause we're not alone—and Umbrella's going down, whether or not we're around to see it happen."

Reston sighed. "Well, you're right about not being around. But as to the rest... you're some of those S.T.A.R.S. people, aren't you? You and your grassroots campaign are nothing to us; you're mosquitoes, an annoyance. And you *will* participate—"

"Participate *this*," he spat, grabbing his crotch. Even through the thick plexi, the gesture was unmistakable.

Vulgar. Young people today, no respect for their betters...

"John, why don't you break out one of those frag grenades?" The other one said coolly, at which point Reston sighed again.

"The walls are plaster-coated *steel*, and the door

will withstand a lot more than you could possibly have. You'd only succeed in blowing yourselves up. It would be a pity—but if you must, you must."

They didn't seem to have a smart reply to that. No one spoke, although Reston could still hear the troubled gasps coming from Cole through the intercom. He'd grown tired of goading them anyway; the surface teams would be putting a call in to control soon, and he really should be there.

"If you gentlemen will excuse me," he said. "I have other business to attend to—like releasing our pets into their new homes. Rest assured, though, I'll be watching your debut; try to make it through at least two of the phases, if you can."

Reston stepped away from the window to the control panel on the left, and punched in the activation code. One of the men started shouting that they wouldn't go through with it, that he couldn't make them—

—and then Reston hit the large green button, the one that simultaneously opened the hatch into One—and released a spray of tear gas into the small anteroom from vents in the high ceiling. He stepped back to the window, interested to see how effective the process was.

Within seconds, a white haze came pouring down from above, obscuring the three men. Reston heard shouts and coughing, and a second later he heard the hatch lock down, which meant they were through. The pressure plates in the floor thus unencumbered, there was a low hiss as the ventilation system kicked on, clearing the room of mist in under a minute.

Nice. He'd have to remember to commend whichever designer had recommended it.

"I'll make a note," Reston said to no one in particular. He smoothed his lapels and turned to walk back to control, excited to see how well the men would fare against the newest additions to the Umbrella family.

ELEVEN

Cole had no choice but to stumble after the killers, choking and nauseous, his heart sick with dread and hate. He'd been abandoned to death by Reston, the man had even encouraged the assassins to kill him— he no longer knew if they even *were* assassins, he didn't know who the "stars" were supposed to be— he didn't know anything except that his eyes were burning and he couldn't breathe.

At least make it fast, let it be fast and painless...

Through the hatch into One, the door snapping closed behind him. Cole fell back against the cool metal, struggling to catch his breath, gummy tears leaking from beneath his closed lids. He didn't want to see them pull the trigger, he'd rather not have to suffer suspense before he died; dying was plenty enough.

Maybe they'll just leave me here.

The small hope that the thought brought him was stamped out immediately as a big, rough hand latched on to his arm and shook him.

"Hey, wake up!"

Cole reluctantly opened his watering eyes, blinking rapidly. The big black guy was staring down at him, looking mad enough to start hitting. His rifle was pointed at Cole's chest.

"Want to explain what the hell this place is?"

Cole shrank against the door. His voice came out in a stammer. "Phase One. F-forest."

The man rolled his eyes. "Yeah, forest, I got *that*. Why, though?"

Jesus, he's huge! The guy had muscles on his muscles. Cole shook his head, sure that he was about to be severely beaten but not sure what the man was asking.

The other one took a step toward the two of them, looking more upset than angry. "John, Reston screwed him over, too. What's your name again? Henry?"

Cole nodded, desperate not to piss anyone off. "Yeah, Henry Cole, Reston told me you were here to kill him and he told me to stand in there, he was just going to lock you guys up, swear to God I didn't know he was gonna do this—"

"Slow down," the smaller man said. "I'm Leon Kennedy, this is John Andrews. We didn't come here to kill Reston—"

"Shoulda, though," John rumbled, looking around them.

Leon went on as if he hadn't spoken. "—or anyone else. We just wanted something Reston is supposed to have, that's all. Now—what can you tell us about this test program?"

Cole swallowed, wiping at the water on his face. Leon seemed sincere—

—and what are your options here? You can get shot, get left behind, or work with these guys. They've got guns, and Reston said the test specimens were designed to fight people and oh shit how'd I wind up in this mess?

Cole looked around at One, amazed at how different it seemed now that he was locked in, how—menacing. The towering artificial trees, the plastic underbrush and fallen synthetic logs—with the subdued lighting and humidified air, the dark walls and painted ceiling, it almost felt like a real forest at twilight.

"I don't know a whole lot," Cole said, looking at Leon. "There are four phases—woods, desert, mountains, city. They're all big, each one's like two football fields, side by side, I forget the exact measurements. Word is that they're supposed to be suitable habitats for these hybrid test animals; they're even gonna stock them with live food, mice and rabbits and such. Umbrella's testing out some kind of disease-control thing, and the test animals are supposed to have similar circulatory systems to humans, something like that, it'll make good study material..."

He trailed off, noticing the look that the two men exchanged when he'd started talking about the test creatures.

"You really believe that, Henry?" John asked, not

looking pissed anymore, his expression neutral.

"I—" Cole said, then closed his mouth, thinking. About the incredible pay and the don't-ask policy. About the questions from whoever was supervising on any given job—

"*Are you happy working here? Do you feel that you're getting paid enough?*"

—and about the prison cells—and the restraints.

"No," he said, and felt a rush of shame at his deliberate ignorance. He should have known, *would* have known if he'd had the guts to take a closer look. "No, I don't. Not anymore."

Both men nodded, and Cole was relieved to see John alter the position of the gun slightly, pointing it away.

"So do you know how to get out of here?" John asked.

Cole nodded. "Yeah, sure. All of the phases have connecting doors, in alternating corners. They're latched shut is all, no keys or anything—except for the last one, Four, it's bolted on the outside."

"So the door we'll want is that way?" Leon asked, pointing southwest. They were in the northeast corner. From where they stood, the far wall wasn't even visible, the fake woods were so dense. Cole knew there was at least one decent-sized clearing, but it would still be a hike to get through.

Cole nodded.

"Can you tell us about these test animals? What do they look like?" John asked.

"I never saw 'em, I was just here to do the wiring— cams and conduits, like that." He looked between the two men hopefully. "But how bad could they be, right?"

The expressions on their faces weren't encouraging. Cole started to ask what *they* could tell *him* when a loud, metallic clattering filled the moist air, like a giant gate being raised. It came from the back, the west wall, where Cole knew the animal pens were kept—

—and a second later, a shrill, piercing shriek cut through the air, a long and warbling note that was quickly joined by another, and another, and then too many to tell apart.

There was a beating sound, too, so huge that for a moment, Cole couldn't place it—and when he did, he felt a little like screaming.

Wings. The sound of gigantic wings beating the air.

* * *

They were fifteen feet off the ground, atop a double row of wooden crates in one corner of the warehouse. Even the slightest movement made them sway a little, which made Claire deeply uneasy.

Not enough that John and Leon are gone, or that we're hiding from a bunch of Umbrella goons. No, we have to be stuck on Mount Precarious in a pitch-black icebox. One of us sneezes too hard and we all go down.

"This sucks," she whispered, as much to break the tense silence as to vent. The helicopter noise had stopped, but they hadn't heard anyone outside yet either.

She was surprised to feel Rebecca's body quaking next to hers, and to hear a muffled giggle; the young biochemist was trying to suppress it, and wasn't having an easy time. Claire grinned, absurdly pleased.

A few seconds passed, and Rebecca managed to say, "Yes. You're so right," and then they were both choking back laughter. The boxes teetered gently.

"*Please*," David said, sounding edgy. He was on top of the second stack of crates, on Rebecca's other side.

Claire and Rebecca quieted down, and again a waiting silence fell over them. They were in the northeast corner, both on their stomachs, handguns pointed toward the wall across from them in the general direction of the other door. David said there were two; he was facing south, covering the one they'd entered by.

The tension-breaking giggle fit had relaxed Claire a little. She was still cold, still afraid for Leon and John, but their situation didn't seem so terrible. Bad, definitely, but she'd been in much worse circumstances.

In Raccoon, I was on my own. There was Sherry to watch out for, we had Mr. X on our trail, we had a shitload of zombies to wade through and were totally lost. At least now I have some idea of what we're up against; even an army of gun-toting creeps isn't as bad as not knowing what's what—

Outside of the warehouse, a noise. Someone

was pulling at the door that she and Rebecca were covering; a quick, rattling shake and then silence again—except Claire thought she heard footsteps now, padding against the ground outside.

Checking doors. And if David's lock-rigging isn't convincing, or they happen to look closely...

At least it was David covering them; he was amazing, cool and efficient, and with as quick a mind as she'd ever encountered. It was like he knew just what to do—instantly, no matter what happened. Even now—David had said that they'd probably be doing a straight-across sweep, starting at one end or the other and checking each building in teams.

Military strategist, no kidding. Claire ran over what he'd told them again, not so much a plan as a what-if list. But still, just having *something* to concentrate on was a relief.

If only one team comes in, three or less, we stay quiet, don't move until they leave, head to the door across from where they entered and wait. When we hear them on the other side, we head out and run for the fence. If they come in and spot us, we shoot; we pick off the others one at a time as they come through the door, then climb down, then run.

If there are two or more teams, wait 'til David throws the grenade and then shoot; same if they've got night-vision, the grenade'll blind 'em. If they manage to return fire, we climb down the back, use the crates as cover—

The other variables disappeared as she heard the

other door being shaken. Shaken—and then kicked.

Thunk!

The door blew open, a square of pale light appearing in the blackness. The bright beam of a flashlight pierced the dark, flitting across a wall of boxes, then turning back toward the door.

A soft *click*—and then a whispered curse.

"What?" A different voice, also whispering.

"Lights are out." A pause, and then, "Well, come on. They're probably in the other one anyway, they didn't get all the way through the lock on this one."

Thank God. Way to go, David. The two were going to search, but they didn't suspect their presence.

A second beam appeared, and Claire could see the vaguest human shapes silhouetted behind the two powerful lights, both of them men by the voices. They started to move forward, the beams dancing over the stacks of boxes and crates.

Stay quiet, don't move, wait. Claire closed her eyes, not wanting for either of the men to feel watched; she'd heard once that that was the trick to hiding. Not to look.

"I'll take south," one of the voices whispered, and Claire wondered if they had any idea how well sound carried in the open space.

We can hear you, numbnuts. A funny thought, but she was scared. At least the zombies hadn't had guns...

The lights split, one heading away from them, the other turning in their direction. It stayed low, at least;

whoever was holding the flashlight apparently didn't realize that people could climb boxes.

Fine by me, just hurry up and get out of here, let us sneak out of this without having to fight! David said that they'd come back for John and Leon when Umbrella had cleared out; he said they'd probably post a guard, maybe two, but that taking out a guard would be a lot easier than taking out an entire squad—

—and a light was shining in Claire's face, the blinding beam hitting her eyes.

"Hey!" A surprised shout from below, and then—

—*bam*, a shot fired, and she felt as much as heard something beneath her give, as Rebecca gasped, as the tower of boxes tipped backwards.

Claire's back hit the wall and she grabbed at the shifting crate they'd been lying on, a chorus of shouts coming from outside, the orange burst of thundering muzzle fire coming from David's weapon—

—and with a shuddering crash, all the crates went tumbling down, and Claire plummeted into the dark.

* * *

When he heard the mighty flap of wings and the shrieking cries, John felt his skin go cold. He didn't like birds, never had, and to run into a flock of *Umbrella* birds, in a sterile, surreal forest—

"Balls," he said, and raised the M-16, pressing the plastic stock tight against his shoulder. Leon's was also pointed up, the ceiling at least fifteen feet above where the tallest trees stopped and painted a deep twilight blue. The trees ranged in height from ten to maybe twenty-five, thirty feet—and at the very top, John saw that there were perching "branches" grafted on, each as big around as a basketball.

Bird's gotta have some pretty big goddamn feet to need that to land on...

The piping screams had stopped, and John didn't hear the beat of wings anymore—but he wondered how long it would be before the birds decided to look for prey.

"Pterodactyls, gotta be," Cole whispered, his voice cracking. "Dacs."

"You're kidding," John breathed, and could see the skinny Umbrella worker shake his head in his peripheral vision.

"Maybe not real ones, it's just a nickname I heard." Cole sounded distinctly terrified.

"Let's head for that door," Leon said, already edging into the false, shadowy woods.

Amen to that.

John started after him, ten, fifteen feet, trying to look up and watch his step at the same time. He tripped almost immediately, one boot kicking against a molded plastic rock, and barely caught himself from going into a full sprawl.

"This ain't gonna work," he said. "Cole—Henry?"

He glanced back and saw that Cole was still huddled against the hatch, his pale, weasely face turned up to the sky.

—ceiling, dammit—

Leon had stopped and was waiting, peering up into the spaced branches. "Gotcha covered," he said.

John walked back, angry and frustrated and seriously uncomfortable; they were in a tight spot, David and the girls could very well be fighting for their lives on the surface, and he wasn't going to waste time coddling some freaked-out Umbrella hump. Still, they couldn't just leave him behind, at least not without making an effort.

"Henry. Hey, Cole." John reached out and tapped his arm, and Cole finally looked at him. His mild brown eyes were positively glassy with fear.

John sighed, feeling a little pity for the guy. He was an *electrician*, for hell's sake, and it seemed that ignorance had been his only real crime.

"Look. I understand you're scared, but if you stay here, you're going to get killed. Leon and I have both had run-ins with Umbrella pets; your best chance is to come with us—and besides, we could use your help, you know more about this place than we do. Okay?"

Cole nodded shakily. "Yeah, okay. Sorry. I just— I'm scared."

"Join the club. Birds give me the creeps. The flying part's cool, but they're so *weird*, got those beady eyes and scaly feet—and have you ever seen a buzzard? They got scrotum heads." John mock-shivered, and saw Cole relax a little bit, even trying on a quivery smile.

"Okay," Cole said again, more firmly. They walked back to where Leon was standing, still watching the air above.

"Henry, since we got the guns, how 'bout you lead?" John asked. "Leon and I will keep watch, and we'll need a clear route so we won't have to worry about tripping over stuff. Think you can handle it?"

Cole nodded, and though he still looked too pale, John could see that he would hold together. For a while, anyway.

Their guide stepped in front of Leon and headed roughly southwest, weaving a crooked path through the strange forest. Leon and John followed, John realizing pretty quick that having Cole lead didn't make much of a difference.

If you don't look where you're going, you're going to trip, John thought wearily, after the sixth time he ran into a fallen "log." *No way around it.*

The Dacs, as Cole called them, hadn't put in an appearance or made any other sound. Just as well; John thought walking through a plastic forest was enough for them to handle. It was a bizarre sensation, seeing the realistic-looking trees and undergrowth, feeling the moisture in the air—but also being aware that there were no smells of earth or growing things, no wind or tiny sounds of movement, no bugs. It was a dream-like experience, and an unnerving one.

John was still edging forward, his gaze fixed on the crisscross of branches overhead, when Cole stopped.

"We're—there's kind of a clearing here," he said.

Leon turned, frowning at John. "Should we skirt it?"

John stepped forward, peering through the seemingly random scatter of trees to the opening ahead. It was at least fifty feet across, but John would rather they go out of their way; being dive-bombed by a pterodactyl didn't sound like fun at *all*.

"Yeah. Henry, veer right. We're going to—"

The rest of his words were lost as that high, warbling screech blasted through the unnatural forest, and a brown-gray shape dove into the clearing and flew at them, extending talons a foot across.

John saw a wingspan of eight or ten feet, the leathery wings tipped with curved hooks. He saw a screaming, toothed beak and a slender elongated skull, flat black eyes the size of saucers, glittering—

—and he and Leon both opened fire as the creature hit the line of artificial trees in front of them, its huge claws gouging into the solid plastic. It held on, spreading its vast membranous wings in a struggle to balance—

—and *bambambam*, holes punched through the thin flesh, streamers of watery blood trickling down from the openings. The animal *screamed*, so close that John couldn't hear the bullets, couldn't hear anything but that quavering, high-pitched shriek— and then it dropped, landing on the dark floor, pulling its wings in—

—and walking toward them on its elbows, like a bat, moving jerkily through the shredded trees, shrieking in short, sharp barks of sound. Behind it, another dropped into the clearing, gusting odorless wind across them as its wide wings folded closed, its long, pointed beak opening and revealing nubs of grinding teeth.

This is bad, bad, bad—

The lurching animal was less than five feet away when John drew a bead on the bobbing head, on the shiny round eye, and pulled the trigger.

TWELVE

The taller one, John, pointed his automatic rifle at the Avl and let loose a hail of bullets. Like a stream of destruction, they hit the Dac's aquiline skull and blew out the other side, dark fluids spattering across the freshly painted trees. Both eyes popped like water balloons.

Damn. Low threshold; it's those hollow bones...

Reston watched as the other gunman pointed his weapon at a second Dac that had landed in the clearing. Even without sound, Reston could see the handgun kick three, four times, hitting the specimen in its narrow chest. The Dac's slender neck curved wildly back and forth, a squiggling dance of death before it sprawled, bleeding, against the ground.

He didn't see any more of the animals touch down, but the three men were retreating, stumbling back into the woods. Poor Cole seemed quite undone, his mouth open in a silent howl, his lank brown hair practically plastered to his head with sweat, his limbs quaking.

Serves him right for not getting to the audio. The lack of sound was annoying, although he supposed the footage wouldn't suffer for it. People knew what bullets and screams sounded like already.

The three were moving out of range, heading west now. Reston switched cameras from the one in the tree to a long shot from the north wall. It was clear that Cole was trying to lead them to the connecting door—although he obviously didn't remember that a second, larger clearing was now in their path. For the moment, though, the Dacs had also pulled back; they generally gravitated toward open spaces. The gunmen had only killed two, which meant that there would be six healthy specimens to greet them in the "meadow."

Reston had released all of the creatures into their habitats just after the call had come on the cell line from a Sergeant Steve Hawkinson, the man who was leading the surface effort. He had informed Reston only that two Umbrella teams—nine men, including himself—were starting a sweep of the compound, and that the fugitives' transport had been spotted; the three were still in the area unless they had a second vehicle, a highly unlikely possibility. Reston told him that the entry's camera had been covered by one of them and asked for an update as soon as anything turned up, then settled in to watch the show.

He poured himself another brandy as he watched the three weave slowly through the trees, John with his weapon pointed above, the other scanning the shadows around them...

He needs a name, too. We have Henry, John, and—Red? His hair is sort of reddish.

Not really, but it would do, just as "Dac" worked for the Av1s. There was no relation to pterodactyls, of course, and the "Av" was for "Aves," birds—and in fact, the Dacs were closer to bats than anything. There were just too many in the mammal series already. At the request of Jackson himself, the specimen growers had added some new classifications for clarity's sake, using some of the secondary contributors to that series's gene pool. Like the Spitters, who were closer to snakes than to goats, but'd been labeled Ca6s, for Capra, because of the cloven hooves...

...and the Dacs do look like pterodactyls, or at least our modern concept of them, Reston thought, looking at the screen that showed the cage entrance. Two of the animals were still inside. The streamlined, muscular body and the narrow beak, the bone "comb" on the top of the head, the fibrous wings... they were really quite elegant in a brutal sort of way. The two in the massive behind-the-scenes "cave" were clearly agitated by all of the excitement, crawling back and forth on their folded wings and swinging their heads from side to side. Reston didn't know much from the biological end, but he knew that they hunted by motion and scent, and that just two of them could take down a horse in under five minutes.

Not so efficient being shot at, however.

It didn't make a difference, really. The Avls had been created for third-world situations, where machetes still outnumbered rifles. It *was* too bad that they died so quickly, the handlers would be disappointed by the loss—but they would have been tested against firepower eventually anyway.

And speaking of...

The three men were getting close to the clearing, moving out of the north camera's view. That would be where the Dacs would make their play. Reston leaned in to watch, realizing that the scenes he was recording would make his career—and that regardless of that fact, he was thoroughly enjoying himself.

* * *

David opened fire as soon as the thug's light found them, hearing the single shot of a weapon down below—

—and felt the splintering of wood to his left, a flurry of splinters spraying his arm. He was too intent on taking out the shooter to stop firing, but he knew with a burst of dread that they were about to fall, that both young women would smash into the concrete if he didn't *do* something—

—and then he was falling, too, the wooden slats beneath him disappearing suddenly, plunging him through the icy dark. David held on to his weapon, pushing his arms out and bending his knees in the half second of blind free fall—

—and then his knees connected with cardboard,

with an unseen box that collapsed beneath his weight, sparing him the worst of it. Instantly he was on his feet, turning toward the other flashlight, which was still shining out from halfway across the warehouse, the first man already down. No time to check on Rebecca, on Claire—the raised shouts from outside were almost upon them.

The torch-bearer went down in the short line of bullets David sent from the M-16, a guided four-foot arc across the darkness behind the light. The flat echoes of the rounds blasted through the alleys between boxes, and as the flashlight dropped, a single grunt of pain and surprise going down with it, David turned the gun toward the open door.

Come on, then—

Rattatattatt—

Submachine gun fire from outside, a sweep across the door... but no one stepped inside. David moved left and sent a burst from his weapon in response, not expecting to hit anyone, the bullets crashing uselessly into the door's frame. He needed to buy them time, even if only a few seconds.

"*Uunh,*" a soft, feminine groan from behind him.

"Rebecca! Claire! Sound off!" He whispered harshly, still watching the pale, empty square of open door.

"Here. Claire, I mean, I'm okay but I think she's hurt—"

Dammit!

David felt his heart skip a beat and he backed up a step, his thoughts racing, a knot of dread in his belly. It had been less than a half-minute since the first shot, but the Umbrella team would have already surrounded the building, if they were any good at all. They needed to get out before the attackers were firmly organized.

"Claire, come to me, follow my voice—I need you covering the door. You see anyone, even a shadow, shoot to kill. Understood?"

He heard her shuffling movements as he spoke and reached out for her as she came close, grabbing hold of her arm.

"Wait," he said, and let another burst from the gun fly, hammering into the wall near the door. He immediately unslung the M-16 and handed it to Claire as the submachine gun returned fire, a rattle of bullets spraying directionless into the dark.

"You can use this?"

"Yeah—" She sounded anxious but steady enough.

"Good. As soon as I say, we're going to start moving for the west door; you'll be covering us."

He was already turning toward the corner, where Rebecca would be. He heard another muffled murmur of pain and fixed on it, moving quickly, dropping to his knees and feeling for the injured girl. He felt silkiness beneath one hand, Rebecca's hair, and ran both hands over her head, feeling for the sticky warmth of blood.

"Rebecca, can you speak? Do you know where you're hurt?"

A cough—and then he felt her fingers touch his arm, and knew she was all right even before she spoke.

"Back of my head," she said, softly but clearly. "Possible concussion, cracked hell on my tailbone, limbs seem okay..."

"I'm going to help you up. If you can't walk, I'll carry you, but we have to go now—"

As if to prove his words, there was another rattle from the gunman outside—

—and a shout that had him moving even before it was finished.

"Fire in the hole!"

David spun, leapt up from his crouch and tackled Claire from behind, calling out, "Close your eyes—" as he closed his own in case of incendiary, praying it wasn't a shrapnel—

—and the *whump* of a grenade launcher, followed by a loud *pop* and hiss that told him it was gas. He moved off of Claire, felt her sit up beside him, heard her ragged, frightened breathing.

God, not sarin, soman, let them want us alive—

Within seconds, David's nose and eyes started to water viciously and he felt a wave of relief. Not nerve gas; they'd used a CN or CS tear gas. The Umbrella team was going to smoke them out.

"West door," David said, and Claire choked out an affirmative, the chemical compound disseminating quickly into the frigid air, an effective but thankfully non-lethal weapon.

He turned back and felt a hand brush across his chest.

"I can walk," Rebecca said, coughing, and David

threw her arm across his shoulders anyway and started for the door, moving as fast as he could through the black. He heard Claire gasping but holding her own, keeping up with them.

David hurried forward, planning as he went, trying not to breathe too deeply. There'd be people at both doors, waiting—

—but how close? They'll want to be right there, waiting to subdue their choking victims...

He had it. As they came to the wall, David fished into his hip bag, pulling out the smooth, round antipersonnel grenade and pulling the pin.

"Claire, Rebecca, behind me!"

Already blind in the dark, the tears only hurt; they didn't interfere with his aim as he pulled his nine-millimeter and swept it in front of him, finding the door.

BAM!

He blew a hole in the door's edge, unlocking it, hearing the surprised cries of the men outside. With hardly a pause, David jerked the door open, *how far to the fence, fifty, sixty meters—*

—and lobbed the grenade, a gentle toss out the door, closing it just as fast as he could, throwing his weight against it and thanking God that it was so very durable—

—and *KA-WHAM*, the door fought with him as the impact fuse went, dirt and shrapnel slamming against it like a wild beast clawing for entrance. David held on, only a second's war but a fierce one nonetheless.

The thundering boom of the M68 gave way to moans and howls of pain, barely audible over the ringing in his ears and the screaming of his breathless lungs.

"Cover to the right and head left!" He shouted, and yanked the door open, whipping the H&K from side to side. The pallid moonlight showed him only three men, all down, all hurt and screaming and still alive beyond the veil of his tears.

Kevlar, full-body maybe—

They'd expect a run to the front, to their escape vehicle, so David turned left. He fixed his wet gaze on the dark fence as Claire and then Rebecca tumbled out behind him, coughing and crying.

"Fence," he said, as loud as he dared, and reached back for Rebecca, sliding his arm around her waist. They stumbled over one of the fallen men, clutching at his bleeding face, and managed a shagging run toward escape, Claire right behind. She sidled quickly after them, the M-16 aimed back toward the front of the compound.

Good girl, we might make this, over the fence and circle away from the van, out into the desert—

They ran, closing the distance much faster than David could have hoped, the fence only ten yards behind the rear of the building they'd been in, the building he'd chosen because of it; the others angled toward the front, too much distance, and the first would have been too obvious—

—then they were almost to the fence when someone fired the machine gun from the darkness behind them, from the cover of the building's other side. At least one of the Umbrella team had fought logic and come around by the unexpected route.

Claire was on it, returning fire, the rapid chatter of the two automatics merging into an explosive duo. The invisible shooter was either hit or ducking as the thundering song went solo, Claire peppering the darkness with the .223s.

Rebecca will need help.

"Claire! Up and over!" David shouted, reaching out for the M-16. She let it go and turned, scaling the fence easily.

"Rebecca, go!" David pulled the trigger and held it, spraying bullets across the cold night, hearing return fire from seemingly everywhere at once, three, maybe four shooters—

—and there was a cry from behind him, from Rebecca, only halfway up the metal grid. A few drops of warmth spattered across David's face and he stopped firing, jumping to catch her before she could let go.

"Got it!" Claire shouted from the other side, and she fired through the mesh, the nine-millimeter rounds pounding and loud, David's pulse even louder. Rebecca was pale, panting harshly, obviously in pain—but she managed to hang on to the fence, even to climb a little as David straddled the fence and lifted her up.

He half-carried her over the top, and as soon as Claire reached up to help, David turned and fired again at the oncoming attackers, still hidden in the shadows, his fury drying the last of the chemical tears.

Bloody bastards, she's still just a girl—

The M-16 went dry and he jumped, then Rebecca was between them, leaning heavily on David's shoulder, and they were staggering out into the freezing desert night.

THIRTEEN

Within minutes of the attack, Leon could see that Cole was in no shape to lead. The Umbrella worker was stumbling blind, headed only vaguely in the direction they needed to go and more from happenstance than by design.

*And now that we know they can attack from the ground...*he and John didn't both need to be watching the skies, so to speak.

"Henry—why don't you let me take over as guide for a few minutes?" Leon asked, glancing back at John. John nodded, not looking all that hot himself; he seemed extremely tight, his gaze darting rapidly back and forth, his hands tight on the M-16.

Maybe he's thinking about the others. About them being "taken."

"Yeah, okay, that'd be—okay," Cole nodded, his relief all too apparent. He wiped at his sweaty brown hair and hurried to get behind Leon, John still in back.

Leon was nervous, but not nearly as frightened as he had been, at least not for the three of them. The birds, Dacs, were unpleasant and dangerous, but it was a relief to have seen them; they weren't as terrible as his imagination had led him to believe upon hearing those first savage cries. Monsters from the mind were always worse than the real thing, and the Dacs weren't even all that durable. As long as he and John were on their guard, they should make it okay.

They were headed due south, so Leon angled them again, realizing that he was starting to catch glimpses of what might be the far wall. The setup was disorienting; the trees were not all that close together, but were scattered so that the woods seemed dense when you looked across it; the thick ground cover, some kind of molded plastic, didn't move underfoot, but there were slopes and rises in the material that made it even harder to get a feel for the size of the chamber.

This is so weird, so over the top—so utterly like Umbrella.

It was like the vast laboratory facility beneath Raccoon, complete with its own foundry and private subway—unbelievable, except he'd seen it himself. And he knew from the ex-S.T.A.R.S. that there'd also been an isolated cove on the Maine coast guarded by teams of viral zombies, and a "deserted" mansion in the woods, the Spencer place—that one had been rigged with secrets, keys, codes, and passages, like the setting for a spy movie that no one would ever buy.

Now this—simulated environments beneath the

barren Utah salt flats. What had Reston called it? The Planet. It was an extravagant, decadent, immoral waste; ridiculous, except—

—*except we're stuck in it, and God only knows what we'll be up against next.*

Leon kept moving, trying not to think about what Claire and the others might be going through. Reston had obviously assumed that the rest of the team had been nabbed, but he didn't *know*. He also didn't know how resourceful Claire and Rebecca were, or how brilliant David was as a strategist. They'd all slipped away from Umbrella before, and there was no reason to think that they wouldn't do it again.

Leon was so intent on the private pep-talk that he didn't see the clearing until they were practically on top of it, less than twenty feet away. He stopped, remembering the last attack—and chided himself for not paying attention.

"Let's back up and go around," he said—and then he heard the beat of wings, and knew it was already too late. In the wilted shadows above the open space, one, two, three of them were diving off perches, soaring down into the rounded clearing.

Shit!

One of them started to screech and then there were others nearby, overhead, hiding in the unlikely trees, who joined in the song, a deafening, horrendous cacophony of needle-sharp sound. Leon fell back, John suddenly at his side, aiming his rifle into the open space.

The first flew at the trees, twisting sideways as if to

fly between them. It pulled up at the last second, so quickly that they didn't get off a shot. As it soared up, Leon saw two on the ground, dragging their sinewy bodies eagerly forward on folded wings.

The noise! It was painful, as shrill and terrible as a thousand screaming infants, and Leon felt the nine-millimeter fire more than he heard it, the heavy metal jumping in his hands. The birds fell silent as the closer of the two took the shot in its curving throat. A ragged hole blew open just above its narrow chest, flaps of gray-brown skin blossoming out like some dark flower. Thin blood gushed from the wound, but the second was already climbing over its spasming body, single-minded in its attack. Leon took aim and—

"Hey hey oh shit—"

Cole's hysterical cry distracted him, the shot jerking right, missing. John opened up on the second Dac, the clatter of automatic fire tearing into the animal. Leon spun and saw Cole stumbling backwards, another of the vicious birds lunging toward him.

How'd it get past us?

Leon aimed, the Dac no more than five feet away from Cole, and even as he pulled the trigger another of the creatures was swooping down from directly overhead. At such close range the nine-millimeter round punctured the bird's chest and blew a fist-sized hole out its low back, the Dac dead before it crumpled to the ground. The newcomer gave one mighty flap, the tips of its huge wings brushing the floor, and flew back up and away.

"Henry, get behind me!" Leon shouted, glancing up—and seeing yet another Dac coming down from a series of perches directly above, tucking its wings in and diving straight for him.

He needed help. "John...!"

The diving bird spread its leathery wings only a few feet from the floor and touched down, surprisingly graceful in its landing. It turned toward Leon and lurched forward. Behind him, he heard the spatter of bullets—and heard it stop, heard John cursing, heard the M-16s aluminum alloy body clatter to the ground.

The Dac in front of Leon opened its long beak and squawked, a burst of angry, *hungry* sound, sidling forward on its bent wings as fast as Leon could back away. The creature was weaving back and forth and Leon didn't have enough ammo to waste, he had to get a clear shot—

—and it *jumped,* a strange, sudden hop that put it only a foot away. With another shrill screech, it bobbed its head forward, its open beak closing on his ankle. Even through the thick boot leather, he could feel the pegs of its teeth, feel the power in its jaws—

—and before he could fire, John was there, he was stamping down on the Dac's snaking neck and pointing his handgun—

—and *bam,* the round snapped its spine, a vertebral knob on its sleek back exploding, shards of pale bone and runny blood spraying outward. It let go of his ankle, and though its neck continued to twist its body was still, bleeding and still.

How many, how many left—

"Come *on*," John called, scooping up the rifle and turning to run. "Get to the door, we have to get to the door!"

They ran. Through the clearing, Cole right behind, the beat of wings behind them, another shrill voice crying into the air. Back into the trees, the lifeless woods, stumbling over branches and veering around the gnarled plastic trunks.

The wall, there's the wall!

And there was the door, a double-wide metal hatch, a deadbolt set low at the right side—

—and Leon heard the terrible screech in his *ear,* inches away, and felt the gust of air across the back of his neck—

—and he let his legs give, collapsing to the ground, and felt sudden pain as something snatched a chunk of hair and ripped it from his scalp, from the back of his head.

"Look out!" Leon screamed, looking up to see the massive bird swooping in on John, almost to the door, Cole beside him.

John turned, not a flinch, not a backward stumble. He raised the handgun and pulled the trigger, a dead shot, and the Dac dropped as if made of lead, its tiny brain suddenly liquid, blowing up and out.

Cole was fumbling with the door, John still aiming over Leon's head, and Leon heard another one screaming as if in a fury, somewhere behind—

—and the door was open—Leon ran, John covering

him as he stumbled after Cole, out of the cool, dark woods and into a blinding heat. John was right behind him, slamming the hatch closed—

—and they were in Phase Two.

* * *

Rebecca was running, out of breath and exhausted and unable to stop, to rest. David and Claire were running with her, holding her up, but she still felt that each step was an effort of pure will; her muscles didn't want to cooperate, and she was disoriented, her equilibrium a mess, her ears ringing. She was hurt, and she didn't know how bad—only that she'd been shot, that she'd hit her head at some point, and that they couldn't stop until they were well away from the compound.

It was dark, too dark to see where the ground was, and cold; each breath was an iced dagger in her throat and lungs. Her thoughts were muddled, but she knew that she'd suffered some brain dysfunction, she wasn't sure what exactly; as she staggered along, the possibilities haunted her. The bullet was easier, she knew by the hot and throbbing pain where it had gone. It hurt terribly, but she didn't think she had a fracture and it wasn't gushing; she was much more concerned about the loss of coherency.

Shot through left gluteal, lodged in ischium, lucky lucky lucky... shock or concussion? Concussion or shock?

She needed to stop, take a temporal pulse, check her ears for blood... or for CSF, which was something she didn't even want to think about. Even in her confused state, she knew that bleeding cerebrospinal fluid was about the worst outcome for a blow to the head.

After what seemed like a very long time, and more twists and changes in direction than she could count, David slowed, telling Claire to slow down, and that they were going to sit Rebecca on the ground.

"On my side," Rebecca panted, "bullet's on the left."

Carefully, David and Claire lowered her down to the cold flat earth, gasping, catching their breath, and Rebecca thought she'd never been more glad to lie down. She caught just a glimpse of the black sky as David rolled her over: the stars were amazing, clear and ice against the deep black sea...

"Flashlight," she said, realizing again how strange her thoughts had become. "Gotta check."

"Are we far enough?" Claire asked, and it took Rebecca a moment to understand that she was talking to David.

Oh, crap this is not good...

"Should be. And we'll see them coming." David said shortly, and he turned on his flashlight, the beam hitting the ground a few inches in front of Rebecca's face.

"Rebecca, what can we do?" he asked, and she heard the worry in his voice and loved him for it. They were like family, had been ever since the cove, he was a good friend and a good man...

"Rebecca?" This time, he sounded afraid.

"Yeah, sorry," she said, wondering how to explain what she was feeling, what was happening. She decided it would be best to just start talking and let them figure it out.

"Look at my ear," she said. "Look for blood or clear fluid, I think I've had a concussion. I can't seem to gather my thoughts. Other ear, too. I was shot and I think the bullet lodged in my ischium. Pelvis. Lucky, lucky. Shouldn't be bleeding much, I can disinfect it, wrap it if you'll hand me my pack. There's gauze and that's good, though, the bullet could've snapped my spine or gone low, chewed through my femoral artery. Lot of blood, that's bad, and me the only medic being hurt—"

As she spoke, David shone the light across her face, then gently lifted and checked the other side before resting her head in his lap. His legs were warm, the muscles twitching from exertion.

"A little blood in your left ear," he said. "Claire, take off Rebecca's pack, if you would. Rebecca, you don't have to speak anymore, we'll fix you right up; try to rest, if you can."

No CSF, thank God...

She wanted to close her eyes, to sleep, but she needed to finish telling them everything. "Concussion sounds minor, explains displacement, tinnitus, lack of equilibrium—may only be a couple hours, maybe weeks. Shouldn't be too bad, shouldn't move though. Bed rest. Find my temporal pulse, side of my forehead.

If you can't, I could be in shock—warmth, elevation..."

She took a breath, and realized that the darkness wasn't just outside anymore. She was tired, very, very tired, and a kind of hazy blackness was encroaching on her vision.

That's everything, told them everything—
John. Leon.

"John and Leon," she said, horrified that she'd forgotten for even a moment, struggling to sit up. The realization was like a slap in the face. "I can walk, I'm okay, we have to go back—"

David barely touched her and somehow, her head was in his lap again. Then Claire was lifting the back of her shirt, dabbing at her hip, sending fresh waves of pain coursing through her. She squeezed her eyes closed, trying to breathe deeply, trying to breathe at all.

"We will go back," David said, and his voice seemed to be coming from far away, from the top of a well that she was falling down. "But we have to wait for the helicopter to leave, assuming that it will—and you'll need time to recover..."

If he said anything else, Rebecca didn't hear it. Instead, she slept, and dreamed that she was a child, playing in the cold, cold snow.

* * *

Desert!

There weren't any animals in sight, they had to be on the other side of the dune, but Cole thought he knew which ones belonged to Phase Two. Before John or Leon could get even a step away, before Cole's ears had stopped ringing from the Dacs' terrible cries, he started babbling at them.

"Desert, Phase Two is a desert so it must be the Scorps, scorpions, see?"

John was pulling a curved magazine from his hip pack, scowling into the artificial sunlight that beat down from above. It had to be at least a hundred degrees in the room, and between the white walls and glaring light it felt a lot hotter. Leon scanned the shining sands in front of them, then turned to Cole, looking as though he'd just eaten something sour.

"Wonderful, that's just great. 'Scorps'? Scorps and Dacs...what are the other ones, Henry, do you remember?"

For a single second, Cole's mind went blank. He nodded, wracking his brain, all of the sweat on his body already evaporated in the bone dry heat.

"Uh—they're, they're nicknames, Dacs, Scorps... Hunters! Hunters and Spitters, the handlers all had these nicknames—"

"Cute. Like Fluffy, or Sweet Pea," John interrupted, wiping his brow with the back of one hand. "So where are they?"

All three of them looked across Phase Two, at the massive sand dune that towered in the middle of the room, glittering beneath the giant grid of sunlamps overhead. Twenty-five, thirty feet high, it blocked their view of the southern wall, including the door in the far right corner. There was nothing else to see.

Cole shook his head, but he wasn't telling them anything; the Scorps were elsewhere, and they'd have to cross the bright and burning sand dune to get to the exit.

"What were the other phases, mountain and city? Have you seen them?" Leon asked.

"Three is like a, whadayacallit, a chasm, on a peak. Like a mountain gorge, kind of, real rocky. And Four is a city—a few square blocks of one, anyway. I had to check the video feeds in all of the phases when I first got here."

John looked up and around, squinting against the harsh light. "That's right, video... do you remember where they are? The cameras?"

Why would he want to know that? Cole pointed left, at the small glass eye embedded in the white wall some ten feet up. "There are five in here; that's the closest..."

With a huge grin, John held up both hands and extended his middle fingers to the lens. "Bite it, Reston," he said loudly, and Cole decided that he liked John, a lot. Leon too, for that matter, and not just because they were the only ticket out. Whatever their motivations, they were obviously on the right side of things; and the fact that they could still joke at a time like this...

"So, we got a plan?" Leon asked, still looking at the wall of yellow-white sand looming in front of them.

"Head that way," John said, pointing right, "and then climb. If we see something, shoot it."

"Brilliant, John. You should write these down. You know, I—"

Leon broke off suddenly, and then Cole heard it. A chattering sound. A sound like nails being tapped on hollow wood, the sound he'd heard when he was fixing one of the cameras only last week.

A sound like claws, opening and closing. Like mandibles, clicking...

"Scorps," John said softly. "Aren't scorpions supposed to be nocturnal?"

"This is Umbrella, remember?" Leon said. "You have two grenades, I've got one..."

John nodded, then said, "You know how to work a semiautomatic?"

The big soldier was watching the dune, so it took Cole a second to realize he was talking to him.

"Oh. Yeah. I haven't ever *used* one, but I went target shooting a couple of times with my brother, six or seven years ago..." He kept his voice low as they did, listening for that strange sound.

John looked directly at him, as if sizing him up— then nodded, and pulled a heavy-looking handgun out of his hip holster. He handed it to Cole, butt first.

"It's a nine-millimeter, holds eighteen. I got more clips if you run out. You know all the gun safety rules? Don't point it at anyone unless you mean to kill, don't shoot me or Leon, all that stuff?"

Cole nodded, taking the gun, and it *was* heavy— and although he was still more scared than he'd ever been in all his thirty-four years, the solid weight of it in his hand was an incredible relief. Remembering what his little brother had told him about safety, he fumbled through checking to see if it was loaded before looking at John again.

"Thank you," he said, and meant it. He'd lured these two guys into a trap, and they were giving him a gun; giving him a *chance*.

"Forget it. Means we won't have to worry about covering your ass on top of ours," John said, but he wore a slight smile. "Come on, let's move out."

John in the lead and Leon behind him, they started east, walking slowly through the changeless environment. The sand was really sand; it shifted underfoot, and with the blasting heat, it made for a real workout.

They'd only gone a short distance when Leon called for a halt.

"Thermal underwear," he muttered, holstering his handgun before pulling off his black sweatshirt and tying it around his waist. He wore a thick, textured white shirt underneath. "I didn't realize we'd be hitting the Sahara—"

They all heard it, only a second before they saw it—before they saw *them*, three of them, lining up at the top of the dune. Tiny rivers of sand trickled down from beneath their multiple legs, each as thick and stocky as a sawed-off baseball bat. They had claws, giant pincing claws that were narrow and black, serrated on the inside, and long, segmented bodies that dwindled to tails, curling up and over their backs—and tipped with stingers. Wicked, dripping stingers at least a foot long.

The trio of sand-colored creatures, each five or six feet long, maybe three feet high, started to chatter— the slender, pointed, tusk-like projections beneath the rounded arachnid eyes tapped against one another, beating out the strange tattoo of clicks that they'd heard before—

—and then all three of the creatures, the *monsters*, were sliding down toward them, perfectly balanced, scuttling through the moving sands with ease.

And at the top of the dune, another three appeared.

FOURTEEN

"Shit," John breathed, not even aware that he'd spoken as he raised the M-16 and opened up.

—*bambambambam*—

—and the first of the scorpion-things let out a strange, dry, *hissing* sound, like air being let out of a giant tire, as the bullets hammered into its curled body. A thick white fluid burst from the wounds that had opened in its insectile face, a face of drooling tusks and spider's eyes, a face with a black shapeless hole for a mouth. Writhing, claws raised, it fell on its side and twisted wildly, digging its own shallow grave in the hot sand.

Leon and Cole were both shooting, the thunder of the nine-millimeter drowning out any more hissing, producing even more of the pus-like blood in the second and third of the Scorps. The white liquid spewed out in *glurts*, like puke, but there were three more of the creatures coming down—

—and the first one, the one that John had drilled full of holes, was getting up. Getting up unsteadily, but getting up all the same. The openings were oozing with that viscous white goo—and even as it took its first step toward them, John saw that the liquid was hardening. Plugging the wounds as efficiently as plaster filled a hole in a wall.

"*Go go go!*" John shouted as the other two creatures, taken down by Leon and Cole, started to move, their wounds already scabbing over. The second threesome was halfway down the dune and closing fast.

Gotta get out.

There were still two more "environments," and they'd already blown at least a third of their ammo; this ran through John's mind in the split-second it took him to spray the Scorps with a hail of bullets, as Leon and Cole ran east.

He didn't even try to take any of the six down, he knew it wouldn't make a difference. The line of explosive rounds was to hold them back until the other two men were clear, his mind grasping for a solution as the impossible animals waved their jagged claws, scrabbling against the shifting sands and spurting more of their bizarre epoxy.

—*grenade but how do I get them all, how do we avoid taking shrapnel*—

The closest of the Scorps was perhaps a dozen feet in front of him when he turned and ran, moving as fast as he could through the blazing heat, his adrenaline up and raging. Leon and Cole were fifty meters ahead, stumbling through the sand, Leon running sideways—watching front and back, sweeping with his semi.

John risked a glance back, saw that the scorpion creatures were still coming. Slower than before but not faltering, their waspish bodies dripping white, their bizarre elongated claws raised and snapping. They were gaining speed, too, faster with each skittering step, a pack of undead bugs looking for lunch—

—*pack, in a pack*—

They might not have a better chance. John dropped the rifle, the sling hanging awkwardly around his neck, and jammed one hand into his pack, still managing a decent run. He came up with one of the grenades, jerked the pin free, and turned, backing up in a shambling jog. He tried to evaluate the distance, the M68's process running through his frenzied mind, the Scorps sixty, seventy feet behind.

—*impact fuse, armed two seconds after it hits, six-second backup*—

"*Grenade!*" He screamed, and threw the round canister up, praying that he'd judged it right as he turned and lunged, the grenade still ascending as he dove into the side of the sand dune.

John swam into it, pushing with all his considerable muscle, burrowing into the hot grit blind and breathless. The sand was cooler underneath, waves of the unpacked stuff pouring across his face, trying to force its way into his nose and mouth, but he couldn't think of anything except pulling his legs in—and what the blast-projected slivers of metal could do to human flesh.

One final, desperate kick and—

—KA-WHAM—

—there was a huge shift all around him, an incredible pressure slamming into him and into the moving wall he was embedded in. He felt the weight on top of him press down, forcing the air out of him, and it took all he had to force one hand up to his face, to cup it over his mouth. Breathing shallowly, he started worming his way back out, wriggling and kicking.

Leon, did they get down in time, did it work—

He fought against the still sliding currents of polished granules, taking one more breath before using both hands to swipe at the heavy sands. In a few seconds he was out, rivulets of grit streaming off of him, his irritated eyes watering. He wiped at them one handed, raising the M-16, looking first at the threat—

—which wasn't a threat anymore. The grenade must have landed right in front of them; of the six mutant scorpions that had been pursuing them, four were in pieces. John saw a still-twitching claw lying across the sand in a puddle of white, a tail with stinger still attached sticking out of the side of the dune, a leg, another leg; the rest was unrecognizable, great hunks of wet mush splattered in a rough semi-circle.

The two Scorps at the rear of the pack were still whole, but were definitely not going to get up again; the bodies were intact, but the eyes and mouth, the strange mandibles, the *faces* were gone.

Blown all to shit, in fact. No amount of white goop in the world's gonna plug that up...

"John!"

He turned, saw Leon and Cole striding back toward him, expressions of amazement on both their faces. John allowed himself a brief moment of completely unchecked pride, watching them approach; he'd been brilliant—timing, aim, everything.

Ah, well. The true soldier takes no accolades for a job well done; it's enough that he knows it...

By the time they reached him, he'd managed to get over himself; thinking about their situation was enough. They were in a psycho testing ground being put through their paces by an Umbrella madman; their team was split up, they had limited ammo, and there was no clear way out of it.

Pretty much, you're screwed. Patting yourself on the back is kinda like giving aspirin to a dead guy; pointless.

Still, seeing the faint hope on the other men's flushed and sweating faces... hope could be misguided, but it was rarely a bad thing.

"There could still be more of them," he said, wiping sand off of the M-16. "Let's get out of here—"

—clickclickclick—

That sound. All of them froze, staring at each other. It wasn't close, but somewhere over the dune, there was at least one more Scorp.

* * *

David had spotted a moving light, maybe a quarter mile southwest of their position, but it had come no closer; if it wasn't for the cold, Claire thought she might feel relieved. The chances of anyone finding them in the endless miles of dark were somewhere near zero; the Umbrella guys had blown it. Even with the helicopter's searchlight—which they apparently weren't going to use—it'd be pure luck if they ran across the three of them...

...although maybe it'd be lucky for us. Maybe they'd have blankets and coffee, hot chocolate, spiced cider...

"How are you, Claire?"

She made an effort to keep her teeth from chattering, but it failed. It had been at least an hour, probably more. "Pretty goddamn cold, David, and yourself?"

"Same. Good thing we dressed warm, eh?"

If it was a joke, she wasn't laughing. Claire snuggled closer to Rebecca, wondering when she'd lose all feeling in her limbs; as it was, her hands were numb and her face felt like it was freezing into a mask, in spite of near-constant changes of position. David was on Rebecca's other side, the three of them huddled together as tightly as was humanly possible, spoon fashion. Rebecca hadn't woke up, but her breathing was slow and even; she was resting comfortably, at least.

That's one of us...

"Shouldn't be much longer," David said. "Twenty, perhaps twenty-five minutes. They'll post a man or two, then go."

"Yeah, so you said," Claire said. "How do you figure the time, though?" Her lips felt like popsicles.

"Perimeter search, perhaps a quarter-mile round—assuming they have six or less men still able-bodied, I'm estimating four—"

"Why?"

David's voice shook with the cold. "Three sent to the back door of the building, two men down inside—and from the sounds, I'd say there were three to seven at the front. Eight or twelve men; any more, and they wouldn't have all fit in the helicopter. Any less, they wouldn't have been able to cover both entrances."

Claire was impressed. "So, why twenty to twenty-five minutes?"

"As I said, they'll cover a certain distance all the way around the compound before they give us up. The size of the compound, tack on a quarter- to a half-mile, and how long it takes an average man to walk a fourth of that distance. We saw that light perhaps an hour ago, and since they most likely would have each taken a direction and searched that single segment... well, twenty to twenty-five minutes. That's including the time it would take to look through the van, as well. That's my guess, for what it's worth."

Claire felt her frozen lips attempting a smile. "You're bullshitting, aren't you? Making it up."

David sounded shocked. "I am not. I've gone over it several times and I think—"

"I'm kidding," Claire said. "Really."

A short silence, and then David chuckled, the

low sound carrying easily through the cold dark. "Of course you are. Sorry. I think the temperature has affected my sense of humor."

Claire alternated her hands, slipping the right one out from beneath Rebecca's hip and sliding the left one under. "No, I'm sorry. Shouldn't have interrupted. Go on, this is really interesting."

"Not much else to say," David said, and she heard the soft, rapid chatter of his teeth. "They'll want to get medical attention for their wounded, and I doubt Umbrella wants one of their helicopters to be seen flying around the salt flats by the light of day; they'll leave a guard behind and go."

She heard him shifting, felt Rebecca's body move as he altered his own position. "Anyway, that's when we'll move. Back to the compound first, a bit of sabotage—and then we'll just see what turns up..."

The way his voice trailed off, the forced good humor in his tone that barely covered the desperation—both told her exactly what he was thinking.

What we've both been thinking.

"And Rebecca?" she asked gently. They couldn't leave her, she'd freeze, and trying to infiltrate the compound again, trying to take out a couple of armed men while carrying an unconscious woman...

"I don't know," David said. "Before she—she said that she might recover within hours, given rest."

Claire didn't respond. Stating the obvious wouldn't help anything.

They fell silent, Claire listening to Rebecca's soft

breathing, thinking about Chris. David's affection for Rebecca was plain; it was like the love between a father and daughter. Or brother and sister. Thinking about him was one way to pass the time, anyway.

What are you doing right now, Chris? Trent said you were safe, but for how long? God, I wish you'd never been assigned to that Spencer place. Or Raccoon, for that matter. Fighting for truth and justice pretty much eats it, big brother...

"Not falling asleep, are you?" David asked. He'd asked her that every time they stopped talking for more than a minute.

"No, thinking about Chris," she said. Forming the words was a chore, but she figured it was better than letting her mouth freeze shut. "And I bet you're starting to wish we'd gone to Europe after all."

"I do," Rebecca said weakly. "Hate this weather..."

Rebecca!

Claire grinned, not really able to feel it and not caring. She hugged the girl as David sat up, digging for the flashlight—and though she was freezing, though they were cut off from their friends, cut off from escape and facing uncertain odds, Claire felt like things were definitely starting to look up.

* * *

The call came just after John blew up six of the Ar12s.

Reston had been wishing for popcorn up until then; the Scorps' defense systems were working just as the projected numbers had suggested, the exo damage repairing even faster than they'd hoped. What they *hadn't* counted on was how very fragile the connective tissue between the arachnid segments actually was.

One grenade. One goddamn grenade.

The desire for popcorn was as dead as the Ar12s. There were still two left, scuttling around in the southwest corner, but Reston no longer had much faith in the 12s—and although that was important information, he wasn't so certain that Jackson would be pleased with him for obtaining it.

He'll want to know why I didn't take away their explosives first. Why I released all of the specimens. Why I didn't call Sidney, at least, for counsel. And no answer I give will be sufficient...

When the cell phone rang, Reston jumped in his chair, suddenly certain that it was Jackson. That ridiculous notion was gone by the time he picked up the phone, but it *had* given him pause—and made him quite glad that his test subjects wouldn't survive Three.

"Reston."

"Mr. Reston—this is Sergeant Hawkinson, White Ground Team One-Seven-Oh—"

"Yes, yes," Reston sighed, watching Cole and the two S.T.A.R.S. people regrouping. "What's happening up there?"

"We—" Hawkinson took a deep breath. "Sir, I'm sorry to report that there was an altercation with the intruders and they've escaped the premises." He said it all in a rush, obviously uncomfortable.

"*What?*" Reston stood up, nearly tipping his chair over. "How? How did this happen?"

"Sir, we had them trapped in the storage building, but there was an explosion, two of my men were shot and three more were critically—"

"I don't want to hear it!" Reston was furious, unable to believe that he had such incompetents working for him. "What I want to hear is that you did *not* just fail miserably, you did *not* just let three people slip past your 'crack' teams, and that you did *not* call to tell me that *you can't find them!*"

There was a moment of silence at the other end, and Reston just *dared* this screw-up to mouth off, to give him any more reason to make his life a living hell.

Instead, Hawkinson sounded properly contrite. "Of course, sir. I'm sorry, sir. I'm going to fly the helicopter back to SLC and bring back some of our new recruits to extend our search parameters. I'm leaving my last three men to stand watch, two at the compound's east and west, the third at the escape vehicle. I'll be back within—ninety minutes, sir, and we *will* find them. Sir."

Reston's lips curled. "See that you do, *Sergeant*. If you don't, it's your worthless ass."

He flipped the talk switch and tossed the phone back on the console, at least feeling as though he'd done *something* to facilitate the process. A good ball-squeeze worked wonders; Hawkinson would crawl over broken glass to get results, which was exactly how it should be.

Reston sat down again, looking at the test subjects as they slogged their way over the sand dune. Cole had a gun now, and was leading them toward the connecting door. Reston wondered if John or Red had any idea how useless Cole was. Probably not, if they'd given him a weapon...

When they hit the top of the dune and started down the other side, the two Scorps finally moved in. In spite of his earlier resolve, Reston watched closely, holding on to a shred of hope—that it would end there, that the men would be stopped. It wasn't that he had any doubt about the Ca6s in Three, they certainly wouldn't survive *those*...

...but what if they do, hmm? What if they do, and they make it to Four, and they find a way out? What will you tell Jackson, what will you tell your guided tour when there aren't any specimens left to observe? Then it will be your ass, won't it?

Reston ignored the whispery little voice, concentrating on the screen instead. Both Scorps were going in fast, claws and stingers up, their lithe, insectile bodies set to attack—

—and all three men were firing, a silent battle, the 12s dodging and feinting, then falling beneath the stream of bullets. Reston's hands were in fists, though he didn't notice; his attention was entirely on the two downed Scorps, waiting to see if they'd be ready to attack again before the men reached the door—

—except John and Red were moving *toward* the animals, pointing their weapons—

—and shooting out the eyes. They did it quickly and efficiently, and although both Scorps were moving again as they headed for the door, the blind creatures could only flail about in the sand. One of them managed to find a target; with a limber curl, it drove its extraordinarily toxic sting into the other's back. The poisoned 12 whipped around and stabbed the first through the abdomen with one jagged claw, impaling it; it writhed weakly, alive but unable to move or see—bound, dying, to its dead brother.

Reston shook his head slowly, disgusted at the wasted time and money, at the millions of dollars and the man-hours that had gone into developing the inhabitants of phases One and Two.

And Jackson will want that information. Once the test subjects are dead and their friends caught, I'll be able to put the right spin on things; with some of our backers coming in, such a poor performance from our "prize" specimens could be costly. Better to know now...

Yes, he'd be able to pull it off. Now Red was unlocking the connecting door that would lead them into Three; unless they had a case of grenades, they would be dead in minutes.

Reston took a deep breath, remembering who was in control, who was calling the shots here. Hawkinson would handle the surface situation, Jackson would be pleased, the three musketeers were about to be blinded, trampled, and eaten. There was nothing to worry about.

Reston exhaled heavily, managing a somewhat uneasy grin and forcing himself to relax into his chair, dialing up the screens that would show him the Ca6 habitat.

"Say goodbye," he said, and poured himself another brandy.

FIFTEEN

From the terrible, baking heat of the blinding scorpion desert, they stepped into the cold shade of a mountain peak. They stayed by the door, surveying their newest crucible, Leon wondering if they'd be facing Hunters or Spitters in this very gray room.

Gray the rock-studded, sharply angled mountain of stone that loomed in front of them. Gray also the walls and ceiling, and the winding path that snaked west, bordering the "mountaintop." Even the scrubby grasses in and around the misshapen boulders were gray. The mountain looked real enough, rough-hewn chunks of granite mixed into cement, dyed to match and sculpted into crags. The overall effect was of a lonely, windswept ridge high on a barren mountain.

Except there's no wind—and no smell. Just like the other two, no smell at all.

"Might want to put your shirt back on," John said, but Leon was already untying it from his waist.

The temperature had dropped at least sixty degrees, already freezing the sweat he'd worked up from Phase Two.

"So where do we go?" Cole asked, his eyes wide and nervous.

John pointed diagonally across the room, south-west. "How 'bout the door?"

"I think he meant which *way*," Leon said. He kept his voice pitched low, just as the others did. No point in alerting the inhabitants to their position; they'd probably be interacting soon enough.

The three of them examined their options, all two of them: take the gray path or climb the gray mountain.

Hunters or Spitters... Leon sighed inwardly, his stomach knotted, already dreading whatever came next. If they made it out, if they found Reston, he was going to give old Mr. Blue a solid ass-kicking. It went against the belief system that had led him to be a cop, but then, so did White Umbrella's very existence.

"From a defensive standpoint, I'd say trail," John said, looking up at the rough surface of the slope. "We could get trapped if we head up."

"There's a bridge, I think," Cole said. "I only did one of the cameras in here, that one—"

He pointed up and right, into the corner. Leon couldn't even see it—the walls were fifty feet high, and their monotone color blended into the ceiling. It created a kind of optical illusion, making the room seem endlessly vast.

"—and I was on a ladder, I could see over, kind of," Cole continued. "There's a gorge on the other side, and one of those rope bridges going across."

Leon opened his pack while Cole was talking, assessing his ammo situation. "How's the M-16?"

"Maybe fifteen left in this one," John answered, patting the curved mag. "Two more full, thirty each... two clips for the H&K, and one more grenade. You?"

"Seven rounds left, three clips, one grenade. Henry, have you been counting?"

The Umbrella worker nodded. "I think—five shots, I fired five times."

He looked as though he wanted to say something else, glancing back and forth between Leon and John, finally staring down at his dirty workboots. John looked at Leon, who shrugged; they didn't really know anything about Henry Cole, except that he didn't belong there any more than they did.

"Listen... I know this isn't really the time or place, but I just want to tell you guys that I'm sorry. I mean, I knew something was weird about all this. About Umbrella. And I knew Reston was a serious asshole, and if I hadn't been so greedy or so stupid, I never would have got you into this."

"Henry," Leon said. "You didn't know, okay? And believe me, you're not the first to be duped—"

"No doubt," John interrupted. "Seriously. The suits are the problem here, not guys like you."

Cole didn't look up, but he nodded, his thin shoulders slumping as if in relief. John handed him another clip, nodding toward the path as Cole tucked it into his back pocket.

"Let's hit it," John said, talking to both of them but addressing Cole. Leon could hear it in his deep voice, a note of encouragement that suggested he was starting to like the Umbrella worker. "Worse comes to worst, we can retreat to Two. Stick close, keep quiet, and try to shoot for the head or eyes—assuming they have eyes."

Cole smiled faintly.

"I'll bring it up," Leon said, and John nodded before stepping away from the hatch and turning left. The chilled air was as quiet as it had been since they'd come into the room, no sounds but their own. Leon brought up the rear, Cole walking slowly in front of him.

The path was grooved, as if someone had run a rake through the cement before it was dry. With the "peak" to their right, the trail extended about seventy feet and then turned sharply south, disappearing behind the craggy hill.

They'd gone about fifty feet when Leon heard the trickle of rock behind them. Loose gravel falling down the slope.

He turned, surprised, and saw the animal near the top of the peak, thirty feet up. Saw it and wasn't sure what he was seeing, except that it was walking, *skipping* down the hill on four sturdy legs, like a mountain goat.

Like a skinned goat. Like—like—

Like nothing he'd ever seen, and it was almost to the ground when they heard a wet, rattling sound erupt from somewhere ahead of them, the sound of a snot-clogged throat being cleared, or a dog growling through a mouthful of blood—and they were trapped, cut off from escape, the terrible sounds coming toward them from both sides.

* * *

Getting back into the compound was remarkably easy. Rebecca needed help getting over the fence, but with each passing minute, she seemed to be improving, her balance and coordination sharpening. David was more relieved than he cared to admit, and almost as pleased with Umbrella's guard, or lack thereof. Three men, two at the fence and another at the van; it was pathetic.

They'd started back as soon as the helicopter had lifted and headed south, stretching frozen muscles as they moved silently through the dark. When they'd come within a few hundred yards, David had left the others for a quick recon, then come back and led the two shivering women over the fence and into the compound. Before they could take out the watchmen, David knew they needed to get to a safe place out of the cold, to go over their procedure and better assess Rebecca's condition; he chose the most obvious of the buildings, the middle structure. It boasted two satellite dishes and a series of antennae, plus a shielded conduit running down one side. If he was right, if it was a communications relay, it was exactly where they wanted to be.

And if I'm wrong, there are two others to check; one will be a generator room, it's bound to have some sort of climate control. I can leave them there and do the sabotage work solo...

They'd scaled the fence from the south, David amazed at how poorly Umbrella had planned for their re-entry. The two men covering the perimeter were stationed at the front and back; as if there was no chance that anyone would enter from another direction. As soon as they were inside, David led them to the far side of the last building in line, then motioned for a huddle.

"Middle building," he whispered. "Should be unlocked, if it's what I think it is. The lights will be on, though. I'll go inside, then signal for you to follow; if you hear shots, get inside as quick as you can. Stay close to the buildings and stay low when we cross. Yes?"

Claire and Rebecca both nodded, Rebecca leaning on Claire; other than a limp, she seemed to be doing well. She'd said she was still dizzy and that her head hurt, but the confused and erratic thoughts that had so frightened him earlier had apparently passed.

David turned and eased along the wall of the structure closest to the fence, hugging the shadows, frequently glancing back to be sure both women were keeping up. They reached the end facing west and slipped around, David first, checking for the west guard's position. It was almost too dark to see, but there was a density of shadow against the metal mesh that marked him. David raised the M-16 and pointed it at him, prepared to fire if they were seen.

Too bad we can't just shoot him now... but a shot would alert the others, and while David wasn't concerned with the fence men, the one posted at the van could be a problem; he was far enough away that he might radio before coming in to check.

These two will be easy enough, but how to approach him? There was no cover if the man at the mini spotted them coming—

That could wait; they had work to do before worrying about the guards. Crouching, David waved Claire and Rebecca across, the M-16 trained on the shadowy figure at the fence. He held his breath as they slipped across the open space, but they managed it with hardly a sound.

As soon as they were across, David followed, his years of training allowing him to move as silently as a ghost. Once they were cloaked by the building's shadow, David relaxed a bit, the worst of it over. They could cross to the middle building in the thick black of the corridor between the structures.

In less than a minute, they'd reached the crossing point. Nodding at the women to stay back, David went across, stopping at the closed door to their destination. He touched the icy metal of the handle and pushed it down, nodding to himself as he heard the tiny *click* of the unlocked door.

It's communications, then; the team leader would have left it open for the men posted, access to a satellite uplink in case we returned. A calculated guess, but a good one.

It was time to pray for a bit of luck; if the lights were on, opening the door would be like a beacon to anyone even glancing in their direction. The guards had been facing away from the compound when he'd reconned, but that didn't mean much.

A deep breath, and David pushed the door open, registering that the light was low as he slid inside and closed it behind him. He leaned against the door and counted ten, then relaxed, inhaling the warm air thankfully as he studied the interior. The warehouse-type structure had apparently been divided into rooms—and the one he'd stepped into was packed with computer equipment, thick cables trailing across the floor and up the walls, dish connectors...

...everything that links this facility to the world outside...

David hit the wall switch, turning off the single ceiling light, and grinning, opened the door for Rebecca and Claire to join him.

* * *

"Back against the wall!" Leon shouted, and Cole did it before he even knew why. The phlegmy rattling sounds seemed to be coming from somewhere ahead—

—and then he saw the creature coming slowly

toward them from behind, making it impossible to retreat, and barely held back a scream. It stopped fifteen or twenty feet away, and Cole still couldn't seem to get a good look; it was just too bizarre.

Oh, Jesus, what is it?

It was four-legged, with split hooves, like a ram or goat, and was about the same size—but there was no fur, no horns, nothing else that even remotely resembled a natural development. Its slender body was coated with tiny reddish-brown scales, like a snake's skin, but dull instead of shiny; at first glance, it looked like it was covered in dried blood. Its head was somehow amphibian, like a frog's—an earless flat face, small dark eyes that bulged out at the sides, a too-wide mouth—except there were pointed teeth sticking up from a protruding lower jaw, a bulldog's jaw, its head also covered in the dried-blood scales.

The thing opened its mouth, exposing only a few sharp teeth, upper and lower, none of them in the front—and that terrible wet rattling sound came from the darkness of its throat, the bizarre call matched by others, somewhere on the other side of the artificial mountaintop.

The call built, going louder and deeper as the thing raised its head, turning its hideous face to the ceiling—

—and in one sudden, jerking motion, it dropped its head and spat at them. A thick, tarry blob of reddish semi-liquid *stuff* flew at them, at Leon, across the wide open space—

—and Leon raised his arm to block it even as John started to shoot, stepping away from the wall and spraying the monster—

—*Spitter*—

—with bullets. The goop hit Leon's arm, would have hit his face if he hadn't blocked, and in response to the hail of clattering rounds, the Spitter turned and *jumped* up the sculpted mountain—in long, easy jumps that took it to the top in seconds, that didn't denote panic or pain or any stress at all. It loped back about twenty feet, then skipped nimbly back down to the ground, stopping in front of the connecting hatch. As if it *knew* it was blocking their escape.

And it didn't even flinch, holy shit—

The multiple cries from just out of sight didn't get any louder, but they didn't retreat, either. The gargling noises stopped, one at a time, the lack of targets giving them no reason; suddenly, it was silent again, as quiet as it had been when they'd entered.

"What the good goddamn was *that?*" John said, grabbing another magazine from his pack, his expression one of total incredulity.

"Wasn't even hurt," Cole whispered, holding the nine-millimeter so tight that his fingers started to go numb. He barely noticed, watching as Leon touched the thick, wet handful of maroon goop on his sleeve—

—and hissed in pain, drawing his hand back as if he'd been burned.

"Stuff's toxic," he said, quickly wiping his fingers on his shirt and holding them up. The tips of the index and middle fingers on his left hand had gone an angry, inflamed red. He immediately stuck his handgun in his belt and pulled the black shirt off, carefully avoiding contact with the acidic ooze, dropping it to the stone floor.

Cole felt sick. If Leon hadn't blocked...

"Okay-okay-okay," John breathed, his brow furrowed. "This is bad, we want out of here as fast as possible... you say there's a bridge?"

"Yeah, goes over the, uh, trench," Cole said quickly. "Like twenty feet across, I didn't see how deep it was."

"Come on," John said. He started walking toward where the path turned out of sight, striding quickly. Cole followed, Leon right behind. John stopped about ten feet short of the turn and backed against the wall again, glancing at Leon.

"You want to cover, or me?" Leon asked softly.

"Me," John said. "I step out first, draw their fire. You run, Henry, right behind him—and head down, got it? Get across, get to the door—if you can, help me out—"

John's face was solemn. "—if you can't, you can't."

Cole felt a by-now-too-familiar rush of shame.

They're protecting me, they don't even know me and I got them into this... if he could do something to return the favor, he would, although he was suddenly quite sure that he'd never be able to even things out; he owed these guys his *life*, a couple times over already.

"Ready?" John asked.

"Wait—" Leon turned and jogged back to where he'd dropped the sweatshirt. The Spitter by the hatch stood as silent and immobile as a statue, watching them. Leon scooped up the shirt and hurried back, slipping a pocket knife out of his pack. He cut off the offending sleeve, letting it fall, then handed the rest to John.

"If you're gonna be standing still, keep your face covered," Leon said. "Since they don't seem to notice bullets, you won't need to see, to shoot. Once we're across, I'll give a yell. And if it's not safe, I'll—"

The rattling, peremptory calls had started up again, making Cole think of cicadas for some reason, the almost mechanical *ree-ree-ree* sound of cicadas on a hot summer night. He swallowed hard, trying to pretend to himself that he was ready.

"Outta time," John said. "Get ready to go—"

He held up the sweatshirt, then—astoundingly—grinned at Leon. "My man, you *must* invest in a stronger deodorant; you stink like a dead dog."

Without waiting for a response, John put the shirt over his head, holding it open at the bottom so he could see the floor. He jogged out into the open, his face down, Cole and Leon both tensing—

—and there was a rapid *patpatpatpat,* and the black material over John's face was suddenly dripping with great strings of the poison red snot, and he jerked his hand at them—

—and Leon said, "Now!" and Cole ran, head down, seeing only Leon's boots sprinting in front of him, a blur of gray rock, his own thin legs as he sprinted. He heard a gurgling cry to his left and ducked down even farther, terrified—

—and there was the *thump* of wood in front of him, and then he was on the bridge, flat wooden slats rippling underfoot, tied with scrawny twine. He saw the vee-shaped gorge underneath, saw that it was *deep*, that it had been dug into the earth beneath the Planet, forty, fifty feet—

—and then he was back on gray land, before vertigo could even occur to him. He ran, thinking of how wonderful it was that all he needed to think about was Leon's boots, his heart hammering against his breastbone.

Seconds or minutes later, he didn't know, the boots slowed, and Cole dared to look up. The wall, the wall and there was the hatch! They'd made it!

"John, go!" Leon screamed, taking a few running steps back the way they'd come, his semi up and ready. *"Go!"*

Cole turned, saw John rip off the black hood, saw the handful of Spitters grouped loosely in front of him, six, seven of them, calling once more. John tore through their ranks, and at least two of them spat, but John was fast, fast enough that only a tiny bit hit his shoulder, at least as far as Cole could tell. The monstrous creatures started after him in their jumping, hopping movements, not as fast but close.

Run run run!

Cole pointed the nine-millimeter in the direction of

the Spitters, ready to shoot if he thought he could get a clear shot, as John hit the bridge—

—and disappeared. The bridge collapsed, and John disappeared.

SIXTEEN

John felt the bridge drop an inch or two about a half second before the ropes snapped. He instinctively put his hands out, still running, thinking he'd make it—

—and then he was falling, his knees slamming into a moving wall of wooden slats, his hands clenching the second they touched solid—

—and all he heard was a *whoosh* sound, and then the knuckles of his right hand crashed into rock, and he was dangling over a very deep chasm, a slat of loose wood in his left hand. He'd managed to grip one of the pieces still attached to the now hanging bridge; both ties that had anchored it to the north side of the rift had snapped.

John dropped the useless slat, hearing it clatter to the bottom of the chasm along with several other pieces that had come untied. He reached up to get a better grip—

—and *thwock*, a gob of red mucous suddenly

appeared in front of him, less than a foot to the right of his face, sliding down the chasm wall in a melting rope.

—shit on toast—

Bambambam, someone was shooting a nine-millimeter, and the rising rattle of Spitters getting ready to spit told him that he definitely needed to get out.

He reached up again, his biceps flexing, straining against the fabric of his sweatshirt as he grabbed one of the slats above and pulled himself up. Above, more shots, closer, and a shout from Leon that was cut off as more bullets thundered.

Kick ass, boys, I'm coming—

Hand over hand was a bitch, particularly with bleeding knuckles and an automatic rifle hanging from his neck, but he thought he was doing pretty well, reaching up for the next handhold—

—and hot wetness hit the back of his right hand, and it *hurt,* it was like acid, burning—

—and he let go, flinging the gelid acid away, wiping at his shirt wildly. He held on to the shuddering bridge with his left, but just barely, the pain like a fire, maddening. It was all he could do to resist his natural instinct, to clutch at the screaming wound— and with the way his fingers were starting to tingle, he thought he might not have that much longer to worry about it.

"He's right here!"

A cracked, hysterical shout from directly above. John tilted his head back, saw Cole crouched at the lip of the chasm, his work shirt pulled up over his nose, his gaze frantic and scared.

"John, give me your hand!" he screamed, and reached down as far as he could, flakes of concrete falling from beneath his sliding boots. If he said anything else, it was lost in another series of explosive rounds as Leon worked to hold the Spitters at bay.

It only took a split-second for John to react to Cole's command, and in that instant he understood that he was going to get out. Henry Cole stood all of five-eight and probably weighed one-fifty sopping wet. With his clothes on. What was more, he looked like some mad turtle hunkered down in the shell of his shirt.

Too goddamn funny. Funny, and touching in an idiotic way, and although his hand still hurt like a son of a bitch, he'd actually forgotten to feel it for a second or two.

John grinned, ignoring Cole's trembling fingers, forcing himself to concentrate on pulling himself up with his injured hand. There were more rattling cries from behind him but no spit-bombs for the moment.

"Tell Leon to use the grenade," he gasped, and Cole turned, shouting over another burst from Leon's semi.

"...says grenade! John says use a grenade!"

"Not yet!" Leon screamed back. "Get clear!"

Thwap-wap, two more globs flew across the chasm, one hitting Cole's boot, the other only inches from John's sweating face.

Put on the power, John—With a final, deeply felt grunt, John grabbed the wood at the very top and pulled himself up, pulled and then was pushing down, bringing his knee up to climb out.

"I'm good, go!"

Cole the mad turtle needed no further incentive. He took off running as Leon continued to cover for John, as John crouch-ran toward him, jamming his injured hand into his pack and pulling out his last grenade—he'd already popped the pin when he saw that Leon had his grenade in hand.

"Do it!" John yelled, reaching Leon, Leon winding back and then lobbing the powerful explosive at the Spitters, throwing high. Then both of them were running, John shooting a look back to see that three, four of the animals had already leapt into the chasm.

No time to think. John threw low, threw as hard as he could, his grenade disappearing into the rift as Leon's landed in front of the others—

—and they were diving and rolling, the blasts almost simultaneous, *KA-WHAM-WHAM*, the sound of powdered rock raining down, an incredibly high-pitched squealing coming from somewhere—

"You got 'em! You got 'em!"

Cole was standing in front of them, a look of unabashed glee and not a little awe on his narrow face. John sat up, Leon next to him, both turning back to see.

They hadn't killed all of them. Two of the four still on the other side of the chasm were mostly intact, alive—but blind and broken, their legs splintered, black fluid obscuring whatever was left of their faces as they squealed in fury, the sound like a guinea pig being stepped on. The other two must have been directly in front of the blast; they were just bleeding, shattered bags, bones sticking up from the liquid piles like—like broken bones. From the man-made gorge there were more of the screaming squeals, and nothing leapt out to attack. For all intents and purposes, it was over.

John crawled to his feet, studying the back of his hand. Contrary to how it felt, the skin hadn't melted off. There were a few small blisters forming and the flesh looked scorched, but he wasn't bleeding.

"You okay?" Leon asked, standing and brushing at his clothes, his youthful features looking a lot less youthful to John.

I'm not calling him a rookie anymore.

John shrugged. "Think I broke a nail, but I'll live."

He saw that Cole was still beaming at them, his body shaking with the adrenaline aftermath; he seemed at a loss for words, and John had a sudden clear memory of how he'd felt after his first battle, the first in which he'd acted bravely. How helplessly elated he'd been. How incredibly *alive.*

"Henry, you're a funny guy," John said, clapping his hand on the smaller man's shoulder and smiling.

The electrician grinned uncertainly, and the three of them started for Four, leaving the furious squeals of the dying animals behind.

* * *

When the dust cleared and the three men were still alive, Reston slammed his fist against the console in anger and rising dread, his stomach lurching, his eyes wide with disbelief.

"No, no, *no,* you stupid shits, you're *dead!*"

His voice was a little slurred, but he was too shocked to give it much notice, too upset. They wouldn't survive the Hunters, he knew that—

—but they weren't going to survive the Ca6s, either.

Reston couldn't believe that they'd made it this far; he couldn't believe that of the twenty-four specimens they'd encountered, all but one Dac had been left either dead or dying. Most of all, he couldn't believe that he'd let it continue, that his pride and ambition had kept him from doing what he should have done in the first place. It wasn't that he was out of his *league,* he was in the inner circle, he was past that kind of insecurity—but he should have talked to Sidney, at least, or even Duvall; not for advice, but to cover all of his bases. After all, he couldn't be held totally responsible if he'd had counsel from one of the other, older members...

It wasn't too late. He'd put a call in, explain his plan, explain that he had some concerns—he could say that the intruders were only in Two, that would help, he could fix the video times later... and the Hunters *had* been tested before, after a fashion, not the 3Ks but the 121s. There had been some loosed at the Spencer estate; from the data recovered, he knew that the three men *would* be killed in Four. Even if they weren't, they wouldn't be able to get out, and with the backup from the home office, he'd be mostly in the clear.

Satisfied that it was the right decision, Reston reached under the console and picked up the phone.

"Umbrella, Special Divisions and—"

—and silence. The smooth female voice at the other end was cut off in mid-sentence, without even a hiss of static.

"This is Reston," he said sharply, aware that a cold hand was settling around his heart, squeezing. "Hello? This is Reston!"

Nothing; then he suddenly realized that the quality of light in the room had changed, brightening. He turned in his chair, hoping desperately that it wasn't what it seemed to be—

—and the row of monitors that showed the surface were all spitting snow. All seven, off-line—and only seconds later, before Reston could even digest what had happened, all seven went black.

"Hello?" he whispered into the dead phone, his whiskey breath hot and bitter against the mouthpiece. Silence.

He was alone.

* * *

Andrew "Killer" Berman was goddamn cold, cold and bored and wondering why the Sarge had even bothered putting anyone on the van. The bad guys weren't coming back, they were long gone—and even if they *did* decide to come back, they sure as hell weren't going to try to get to their vehicle. It'd be suicide.

Either they had a backup car or they're frozen solid out on the plain somewheres. This is total bullshit.

Andy pulled his scarf up around his ears, then readjusted his grip on the M41. Fifteen pounds of rifle didn't sound like much, but he'd been standing for a long goddamn time. If the Sarge didn't get back soon, he was going to get into the van for a while, rest his feet, get out of the cold; they weren't paying him enough to freeze his balls off in the dark.

He leaned against the back bumper and wondered again if Rick was okay; he didn't really know the other guys who'd been cut up by the frag, but Rick Shannon was his bud, and he'd been all bloody when they'd loaded him into the 'copter.

Those assholes come back here, I'll show 'em bloody...

Andy sneered a grin, thinking that they didn't call him Killer for nothing. He was an excellent goddamn shot, best on his team, the result of a lifetime of deer hunting.

And also cold, bored, tired, and irritable. Dumbass duty. If the trio of dickheads showed up, he'd eat his own hat.

He was still thinking that when he heard the soft, pleading voice come out of the dark.

"Help me, please—don't shoot, please help me, I've been shot—"

A breathy, feminine voice. A *sexy* voice, and Andy grabbed his flashlight and turned it out into the black, finding the voice's owner not thirty feet away.

A girl, dressed in tight black, stumbling toward him. She was unarmed and injured, favoring one leg, her pale face open and vulnerable beneath the bright light.

"Hey, hold it," Andy said, although not too harshly. She was *young*, he was only twenty-three but she looked even younger, just legal maybe. And a nicely stacked legal, at that.

Andy lowered the machine gun slightly, thinking how nice it would be to help out a lady in distress. She might be with the three criminals, probably was, but she obviously wasn't a threat to *him*; he could just hold on to her until the helicopter came back. And maybe she'd be grateful for the help...

...and hey, playing the hero's a good way to earn points, big time. Nice guys might finish last, but they certainly get laid an awful lot along the way.

The girl limped up to him and Andy turned the flashlight away from her face, not wanting to blind her. Putting just the right note of sincerity into his voice—chicks dug that shit—he took a step toward her, holding one hand out.

"What happened? Here, let me help—"

A dark, heavy thing slammed into him from the side, hard, knocking him to the ground and knocking the wind right out of him. Before he even knew what happened, a light was shining in *his* face, and the

M41 was being pried out of his hands as he struggled to breathe.

"Don't move and I won't shoot," a man said, a Brit, and Andy felt the cold muzzle of a gun against the side of his neck. He froze, not daring to move a muscle.

Oh, shit!

Andy looked up, saw the girl holding the rifle, *his* rifle, gazing down at him. She didn't look so helpless anymore.

"Bitch," he snarled, and she smiled a little, shrugging.

"Sorry. If it's any consolation, your two friends fell for it too."

He heard another woman's voice from behind him, soft and amused. "And hey, you get to warm up. The generator room's nice and toasty."

Killer was not amused, and as they pulled him to his feet and started marching him toward the compound, he swore to himself that it was the last time he'd ever underestimate a chick—and while he didn't have plans to eat his own hat, he was certainly going to remember this the next time he thought he was bored.

SEVENTEEN

Phase four was indeed a city, and Leon decided that it was the weirdest thing he'd seen so far, hands down. The first three phases had been bizarre, unreal, but they'd also been obviously fake—the sterile woods, the white walls of the desert, the sculpted mountain. At no point had he forgotten that the environments were manufactured.

This, though... it's not some counterfeit organic habitat; this is how it's supposed to look.

Four was several square blocks of a city at night. A town, really, none of the buildings over three stories, but it *was* a town—streetlights, curbs, stores and apartment houses, parked cars and asphalt streets. They'd stepped off of a mountain and into Hometown, U.S.A.

There were only two things wrong with it, at least at first glance—the colors and the atmosphere. The buildings were all either brick red or a kind of dusky tan color; they looked unfinished, and the few parked cars that Leon could see all seemed to be black; it was hard to tell in the thick shadows.

And the atmosphere...

"Spooky," John said quietly, and Leon and Cole both nodded. Backs against the door, they surveyed the silent town and found it completely unnerving.

Like a bad dream, one of those where you're lost and you can't find anyone and everything feels wrong...

It wasn't like a ghost town, it didn't have the air of an abandoned place, a place that had outlived its usefulness; no one had ever lived there, no one ever would. No cars had driven down its streets, no children had played on its corners, no *life* had called it home... and the blank, unlife feeling was—spooky.

The hatch had opened up onto a street that ran east to west, dead-ending just to their left in a wall painted midnight blue. From where they stood, they could see all the way down one wide, paved road that went south, ending in darkness some indeterminate distance ahead, a grid of intersecting streets along the way. The soft light from the streetlamps cast long shadows, just bright enough to see by and too dark to see clearly.

There was a car just in front of them, parked in front of a tan two-story structure. John walked across to it and rapped on its hood. Leon could hear the hollow *tink* sound beneath his hand; an empty shell.

John walked back, scanning the shadows warily.

"So... Hunters," he said, and Leon had a sudden

realization that was almost as freaky as the lifeless blocks stretched out in front of them.

"The nicknames are all descriptive," he said, ejecting the clip from his semi to count the rounds. Five left, and only one more full mag, though John still had a couple—no, he only had one, Cole had the other. And unless Leon was mistaken, John only had one full magazine left for the M-16; thirty rounds, and whatever was still in the rifle.

No more grenades, almost out of ammo…

"So?" Cole asked, and John answered, his gaze narrowing as he spoke, his expression even more watchful as he searched the heavy darkness of every corner, every window.

"Think about it," John said. "Pterodactyls, scorpions, spitting animals… Hunters."

"I—oh." Cole blinked, looking around them with new fear. "That's not good."

"You say the exit's bolted?" Leon asked.

Cole nodded, and John shook his head at the same time.

"And like an asshole, I used the last grenade," he said softly. "No chance at blowing the door."

"If you hadn't, we'd be dead," Leon said. "And it probably wouldn't have worked anyway, not if it's the same kind of setup as the entrance."

John sighed heavily, but nodded. "Guess we can burn that bridge when we come to it."

They were all quiet for a moment, a profoundly uncomfortable silence that Cole finally broke.

"So... ears and eyes open and stick close," he said tentatively, a question more than a statement.

John raised his eyebrows, smirking. "Not bad. Hey, what are you doing with your life if we make it outta here? Want to join the cause, stick it to Umbrella?"

Cole grinned nervously. "If we make it out, ask me again."

As ready as they were going to be, they started south, walking slowly down the middle of the street, the dark buildings watching them with blank glass eyes. Although all of them tried to move quietly, the empty town seemed to echo back the soft sounds of their boots on asphalt, even their breathing. None of the buildings had signs or decorations, and there were no lights inside as far as Leon could tell. The oppressive, lifeless feeling gave him an unpleasant flash of the night he'd driven into Raccoon for his first day on the RPD, after Umbrella had spilled their virus.

Except the streets there smelled like death and cannibals roamed through the dark, crows were feeding on corpses, it was a city in its death throes...

About midway down the block, John held up one hand, snapping Leon back to the present.

"Just a sec," he said, and jogged over to one of the "stores" on the left, a glass-fronted construct that reminded Leon of a pastry shop, the kind that always had wedding cakes in their windows. John peered in through the glass, then tried the door. To Leon's surprise, it opened; John leaned inside for a long second, then closed it and jogged back.

"No counters or anything, but it's a real room," he said, his voice low. "There's a back wall and a ceiling."

"Maybe the Hunters are hiding out in one of them," Leon said.

Yeah, more scared of us than we are of them, wouldn't that be nice. We should be so lucky—

"That's it!" Cole said too loudly, then immediately dropped his voice, flushing. "How we can get out, maybe. The, uh, animals were all kept in cages or kennels or something behind the back walls. I don't know about the other phases, but there's a hall that runs around Four, I've seen the door to this one's, it's maybe twenty feet from the southwest corner. It has to be easier than the exit; I mean, it'd be locked, but probably not reinforced."

John was nodding, and Leon thought it sounded a hell of a lot more plausible than trying to get through a hatch bolted from the outside.

"Good," John said, "good call. Let's see if we can—"

Something moved. Something in the shadows of a tan two-story building on the right, something that shut John up and had all of them aiming into the darkness, tense and alert. Ten seconds passed, then twenty—and whatever it was seemed to be holding perfectly still. Or...

...or, we didn't see anything at all.

"Nothing there," Cole whispered, and Leon started to lower the nine-millimeter uncertainly, thinking that it had *looked* as though something was moving—

—and then the something they couldn't see

screamed, a shrill and terrible shriek like some kind of terrible bird, like a feral beast in a blind rage—

—and the darkness itself moved—Leon still couldn't see it clearly, it was like a shadow, a part of a building that was in motion, but he saw the tiny, shining eyes, light-colored and at least seven feet off the ground, and the dark and ragged talons that nearly touched the asphalt, and he realized that it was a chameleon as it sprang toward them, still screaming.

* * *

Reston hurried back toward the control room, the weight of the sidearm against his hip making him feel a little better. He'd feel better still if he made it back in time to watch the Hunters slaughter the three men, although he'd settle for just seeing the dead bodies.

That would be perfectly fine, no problem so long as they die.

Reston wanted a drink, he wanted to get back to control, lock himself in and wait for Hawkinson to come back. He'd felt a moment of near-hysteria when he'd realized that communications had gone down, but nothing had changed, not really. The elevator was still locked off and the incompetent sergeant would be back with the helicopter in no time at all; if it *was* the surface trio who'd cut the outside lines—which he had no doubts about, not really—Hawkinson would handle them. If by some small chance it was actually a technical problem, a new electrician would be brought in as soon as he missed his morning report.

Not being able to contact his colleagues had been the distressing part, but he'd decided that it could work to his advantage; who wouldn't be impressed, that in such nerve-wracking circumstances he'd still managed to handle things? All things considered, trapping the invaders in the test program was his only recourse. No one would blame him, or at least not overly much.

Retrieving the .38 revolver from his room had eased his mind even more; he'd brought it to the Planet mostly because it had been a gift from Jackson, and though he knew very little about guns, he knew that all he had to do with the .38 was pull the trigger. The heavy handgun practically shot itself, there wasn't even a safety switch to fuss with...

Reston was halfway back to control when it occurred to him that he should have let the workmen out of the cafeteria; he'd walked right past the locked door, twice, and hadn't thought of it. Too much brandy perhaps. He considered going back for about one heartbeat, deciding that they could damn well wait; making certain that the 3Ks were acting as they should was much more important. Besides, he meant to fire the whole worthless lot as soon as he'd reestablished contact with the home office; not one of them had even tried to protect the Planet or their employer.

Control, ahead on the right. Reston broke into a jog, rounding the corner to the offshoot and hurrying through the door. There was movement on one of the screens, and he ran to the chair, both excited and anxious to see the men fall. It was nothing to be ashamed of, they *were* in the wrong, after all—

—and they weren't dead, not one of them, but Reston saw that now it was only a matter of moments. All three men were shooting at one of the Hunters, and as he watched, a second loped on to the scene, still as black as the car it must have been standing by.

Red spun to his right, shooting at the new threat, but the 3K wasn't to be put off by a few puny bullets; with a single massive leap, the Hunter closed the gap between them, twenty feet with one powerful thrust. They could do almost thirty, Reston knew from the preliminary data—

—and now Cole was firing at it, too, as John continued to blast at the first, already the deep gray of the asphalt. The first had taken a lot, fire from all three men; as Reston watched, it turned and sprang off of the screen, out of sight.

The second was still a deep shining black, perfectly defined as it raised one muscular arm to swat at the bullets hammering its body. Huge, a naked, sexless humanoid shape, the towering beast with the sloping, reptilian skull and three-inch talons threw back its head and howled. Reston knew the sound, his mind filling it in for the silently screaming creature as it started to disappear into the street, the match near perfect, as it swung its arm again and Red was knocked sprawling.

Yes!

John stepped in front of his fallen comrade and

blasted at the fading monster, as Cole pulled Red to his feet, the two men backing away. There was some vocal interchange—

—and the two ran off the screen, headed south... had the creature been hurt? John stopped firing and there was blood pouring from somewhere, covering the 3K's face, its chest—

—*eyes, must have hit its eyes. Dammit!* It reeled and fell, not a fatal wound but one that would incapacitate it for a while.

John turned and ran after his companions, no other Hunters in sight—at least Reston didn't think so. Not that it mattered, they were as good as dead; there was no way they could get through the city without being attacked, nowhere they could hide— though just to be on the safe side, Reston tapped the doorlock for the connecting door back to Three.

No retreat, gentlemen....

They hadn't appeared on the screen that showed the street just south of the first camera angle; frowning, Reston switched cameras, using one from a building front—

—and saw a door close, the men seeking sanctuary inside one of the stores. Reston shook his head. That would probably shield them for five minutes, certainly no longer; the 3Ks had the strength to tear down the city, if they so chose, and hunted primarily by sense of smell. They'd track the cowering men, track them and finally put an end to their troublemaking, useless lives.

There wasn't a camera in the building they'd

entered; he'd have to wait for them to reappear, or for the Hunters to drag them out. Reston grinned, his teeth grinding together, impatient, wondering why the 3Ks were taking so goddamn long. It was time for the test to end, time for the Planet to be restored.

The Hunters wouldn't fail him. He just had to wait a few more minutes.

* * *

They found the way in at the back of the middle building, past the generator room, where they'd put the three snarling guards. It was a total fluke, as they'd only been looking for the controls to unlock the service elevator back in the entry building.

There were four of them, a bank of elevators in a carpeted alcove against the far west wall. They weren't operational, but there was a two-man lift in the first shaft they opened up, David and Claire prying the doors open with no small effort. Though tired and unwell, the sight of the tiny platform hooked to its own pulley system made Rebecca want to laugh out loud.

They'll never suspect that we're coming, we'll slip in like shadows.

"Looks as though someone forgot to lock the back door," David said, a look of triumph on his weary face.

Claire looked at the small square of metal doubtfully. "Will we all fit?"

David didn't answer right away, turning to look at Rebecca. She knew what he was going to suggest and started digging for a decent argument before he even opened his mouth.

The helicopter could come back, probably will, if they're injured you'll need me, what if the guards manage to get out—

"Rebecca—I need an honest assessment of your condition," he said, his features carefully neutral.

"I'm tired, I have a headache and a limp—and you need me down there, David, I'm not a hundred percent but I'm not on the verge of collapse, either, and you said yourself that another team is probably on the way—"

David was smiling, holding up his hands. "All *right*, we all go. It will be a tight fit, but the weight shouldn't be a problem, you're both small..."

He stepped inside, pulling his flashlight and shining it across the hanging cables, then on the simple control box attached to the lift's half-railing. "...I think we can manage well enough. Shall we?"

Rebecca and then Claire stepped into the elevator shaft, the makeshift service platform only filling a quarter of the dark space. Cold, open air was above and below, and the rail was only on one side. Claire squirmed uncomfortably against the metal bar; the three of them were pressed tightly together.

"Wish I had a breath mint," Claire muttered.

"*I* wish you had breath mint," Rebecca said, and Claire snickered. Rebecca could feel the movement of Claire's rib cage against her arm; they were packed in tight.

"Here we go," David said, and pushed the controls.

The lift started to descend with a huge, buzzing rumble that was so loud Rebecca began having second thoughts about their sneak attack. It was slow, too, inching down at less than half the speed of a normal elevator.

God, this could take forever...

Just the thought made Rebecca feel incredibly weary, the noise of the roaring motor compounding her headache. Standing still made her realize just how sick she really felt, and as the bright square of the open doors slid up, shrinking away as they descended into the dark, Rebecca was suddenly glad that they were huddled together; it gave her an excuse to lean heavily against David, her eyes closed, trying to keep herself together for just a little longer.

EIGHTEEN

They were in trouble, falling into the building and moving to the back wall through the dark, sweating and gasping, Cole expecting the flimsy door to crash open any second.

—boom, and they come pouring in, screaming, clawing us to shreds before we even see them—

"Got a plan," John panted, and Cole felt a flicker of hope, a hope that lasted until John's next sentence.

"We run like hell for the back wall," he said firmly.

"Are you nuts?" Leon said. "Did you see that one *jump*, there's no way we can outrun them—"

John took a deep breath and started talking, low and fast. "You're right, but you and I are both good shots, we could take out some of the streetlights along the way. Even if they can see in the dark, it'll be a distraction, stir up some confusion maybe."

Leon didn't say anything, and although he couldn't see his face clearly, Cole saw him rubbing at his shoulder where the creature had smacked him. Slowly, like he was actually considering John's idea.

They're both nuts!

Cole struggled to keep the blatant terror out of his voice. "Isn't there some other option? I mean, we could... we could climb, go across on the rooftops."

"Buildings are all different heights," John said. "And I don't think they're built to hold much weight."

"What if we—"

Leon interrupted softly. "We don't have the ammo, Henry."

"So we go back to Phase Three, think it over..."

"We're closer to the southwest corner," John said, and Cole knew they were right, knew it and hated it, a lot. Still, he searched for some other option, trying to think of some other way. The Hunters were terrible, they were the most terrible things Cole thought he'd ever seen—

—and from somewhere outside, one of them screamed, the screeching, furious sound blasting through the thin walls, and Cole realized that they didn't have time to come up with a better plan.

"Okay, yeah, okay," he said, thinking that the very least he could do would be to suck it up and face the inevitable like he actually had guts.

I won't drag them down, he thought, and took a deep breath, straightening his shoulders a little. If this was the way it had to be, he wasn't going to shame himself in front of them by turning into a sniveling coward—and he wasn't going to lower their chances by becoming a burden.

Cole pulled the clip that John had given him out of his pocket and fumbled through swapping it for the empty, his heart pounding—and was a little surprised to find that now that he was committed, that the decision was made, he felt stronger, braver.

I might very well die, he said to himself, and waited for the rush of horror—but it didn't come. He'd already be dead if it wasn't for John and Leon, and maybe this would be his chance to keep one or both of them from getting hurt.

Without another word, the three of them moved for the door, Cole thinking that his life had changed more in the last couple of hours than in the last ten years— and that in spite of how it had come about, he was glad for the change. He felt whole. He felt *real*.

"Ready..." John said, and Cole took a deep breath, Leon grinning at him in the soft light from the window.

"...*now!*"

John yanked the door open and they ran out into the street as all around them, the night was shattered by the savage screams of the Hunters.

* * *

Reston's eyes glittered. He leaned forward, staring at the screen intently, delighted by the suicidal decision. All three of them, storming out into the dark like lunatics. Like dead men who didn't have the sense to stop moving.

They ran south, John in the lead, Red and Cole right behind. From a sidewalk to their right, a Hunter leapt out to greet them—

—and there was a flash of light, a brilliant burst of white-orange high above, burning glass like glitter raining down across the street. One of the street-lamps, they'd shot out one of the lamps, and the 3K seemed to go mad as the broken glass pelted down over it. The red-turning-gray Hunter whipped its body around, frenzied and screaming, searching for its attacker—

—and completely ignored the running men. All three were sprinting past, raising weapons, firing into the sky. Firing at more of the lights, and Reston saw another Hunter spring out into the street, almost lost as a shadow among shadows—

—and Cole, Henry *Cole* feinted left then right, slamming the barrel of his gun against the crouching 3Ks head—

—and there was a burst of liquid, of brain and blood projectile gushing from its temple, the electrician firing at point blank range. The Hunter's arms and legs were spasming, flailing, but it was already dead. Cole jumped away and kept running, catching up to the others as more of the streetlights exploded, glass flying from strobing flashes of white light.

"No," Reston whispered, unaware that he'd spoken, but quite aware that things were going horribly wrong.

* * *

John ran, paused to fire, ran again. The violent shrieks chased them, the rain of glass and smell of burning metal was coming at them from everywhere—

—and he saw one of them in the street, in front of them at the intersection that would take them to the cage, saw the strange flashing eyes and the open black hole of its screaming mouth—

—*save the ammo Jesus it looks just like the street*—

—and he kept running straight at it, taking aim, the thundering rounds of the nine-millimeters behind him, the screaming monster less than ten feet away when he fired.

Now!

A short burst, measured, directly into the howling, unnatural face—

—and it didn't go down, and although he swerved to avoid it, he didn't get far enough. Its screeching face seeming inches from his, visible, thick with blood, it swung one impossibly long arm out and slammed it into John's chest.

The blow crashed into his left pectoral, and John expected to be crushed, thrown through the air, his body shattered—but the creature must have been weakened by the bullets, disoriented, blinded perhaps, because though he could feel his pec contracting in pain—the strike had been brutally solid—he'd taken harder punches. He'd staggered but didn't fall, then he was past and turning left, headed west.

He shot a look back, saw the others still with him, looked ahead—

—there it is!

The street ended at the painted wall less than a block ahead—and there was an opening set about five feet off the ground, a hole eight feet wide and at least ten feet high—

—and there was another scream to his right, he couldn't see the camouflaged Hunter but *bam-bam*, Leon or Cole shot at it, the shriek going frantic with rage. John raised the M-16 and took out another streetlight, *ten seconds and we're there—*

—and a panel of deep blue wall started to slide down over the opening, slow but steady. In seconds, there'd be no escape.

* * *

Reston stabbed frantically at the kennel lock, the gate creeping down on its tracks like a goddamn snail, his hands clammy with sweat, his drunken mind reeling with disbelief.

No no no no—

He'd closed Two and Three but there'd been a Hunter still inside before, he'd left it open, forgotten— and now the animal was gone and the three men were about to get away. To get away from *him*, from the deaths assigned to them.

Faster!

John was shooting a look back, screaming, Red right behind, Cole almost at his side—

—and there was a Hunter less than twenty feet

behind them, gaining ground, its massive body flickering between tan and asphalt, its claws scraping gouges in the street.

Kill them, do it, jump, kill!

John made it to the opening, hands hitting the bottom, vaulting him through in a graceful blur. One hand shot out and Red was there, grabbing it, being jerked inside in an instant—

—and there was Cole, and he was going to make it through, too, the gate wouldn't close in time and there were hands reaching out to him—-

—and then the Hunter behind him swept its arms down, its talons ripping into Cole's back, through the shirt and skin, through muscle, perhaps through bone.

The others swept Cole inside as the gate settled closed.

* * *

Cole didn't scream as they set him down, though he must have been in agony. They placed him on his stomach as gently as they could, Leon feeling sick with sorrow when he saw the shredded mess that had been Cole's back.

Dying, he's dying.

In seconds, he lay in a pool of his own blood. Through the tatters of his wet, crimson shirt, Leon could see the ripped flesh, the torn muscle fibers and the slick shine of bone beneath. The crushed bone.

The damage had been done in two long, ragged tears, each starting above the shoulder blades and ending at his lower back. Mortal wounds.

Cole was breathing in low, shallow gasps, his eyes closed, his hands trembling.

Unconscious. Leon looked at John, saw the stricken expression, looked away; there was nothing they could do for him.

They were in a giant mesh cage that stank of wild animal at the end of a long cement hall, one that apparently ran the length of the four testing areas. It was dark, only a few lights on, revealing the kennel in shadows; the cages were separated by partition walls with huge windows, and Leon could just see the one next to them, the Spitters' home. It was covered in thick, clear plastic, the floor littered with bones.

The Hunters' cage was empty, at least thirty feet wide and twice as long, a couple of low troughs at the mesh walls. It was a cold and lonely place to die, but at least he was out, he wasn't feeling any—

"Turn... me, over," Cole whispered. His eyes were open, his lips quivering.

"Hey, lie easy," John said gently. "You're gonna be fine, Henry, just stay where you are, don't move, okay?"

"Bull, shit," Cole said. "Roll me over, I'm, dying..."

John locked gazes with Leon, who nodded reluctantly. He didn't want to cause Cole any more pain, but he didn't want to refuse him; he was dying, they should give him anything they could.

Carefully, slowly, John lifted Cole and turned him.

Cole moaned when his back touched the floor, his eyes wide and rolling, but seemed to feel some relief after a moment. Maybe the cold... or maybe he was past the point of pain, going numb.

"Thanks," he whispered, a blood bubble popping on his pale lips.

"Henry, try to rest now," Leon said softly, wanting to cry. The man had tried so hard to be brave, to keep up with them...

"Fossil," Cole said, his gaze fixing on Leon's. "In, tube. Guys said—if it got, out, it'd—destroy every. Thing. In the... lab room. West. Understand?"

Leon nodded, understanding perfectly. "An Umbrella creature in the lab room. Fossil. You want us to let it out."

Cole closed his eyes, his waxy face so still that Leon thought it might be over—but he spoke again, quietly enough that they had to lean in to hear him.

"Yeah," he breathed. "Good."

Cole took one last breath, letting it out—and his chest didn't rise again.

* * *

Within minutes of Cole's death, the two men figured out how to escape from the Hunter cage. Reston stared at the screen, feeling nothing, determined not to be surprised. They simply weren't human, that was all; once he'd accepted that, there was nothing to be surprised at any longer.

The feeding troughs had been wedged firmly into long, narrow gaps in the steel mesh so that the handlers could feed the specimens without entering the cage; enough of the trough was outside so that one could simply drop food in, the animals taking it from their side. That the 3Ks might try to pull the feeding containers inside or push them out wasn't a concern, since the gaps were much too narrow for their bodies.

But not for human bodies... or for theirs, whatever they are.

John and Red both started to kick at the trough, and as it started to edge out, Reston picked up his revolver and stood, turning away from the screens. There was no point in watching. He'd failed, the Planet's tests had proved too easy and he would be severely disciplined for what he'd done, perhaps killed. But he wasn't ready to die, not yet—and not at their hands.

But the elevator, the surface people...

It wasn't safe to go up, either. The compound was probably overrun with these S.T.A.R.S. soldiers by now, they'd cut him off and now were just waiting for their two boys to drive him out...

Can't go up, can't kill them, not enough time... the cafeteria!

His employees would help him. Once he freed them, once he explained things, they'd rally around him, protect him from harm. The specifics would have to be edited, of course, but he could work that out on his way.

Have to go now, they'll be out soon, out and looking for me. Looking to avenge Cole, perhaps. Looking to make me sorry, when I only did my job, what any man would do...

Somehow, he doubted they'd understand. Reston walked out, already working through his story, wondering how things had gone so terribly awry.

NINETEEN

From the kennel, they stepped out into a clean and sterile hallway and turned left—west—moving quickly through the deserted corridor. Neither of them spoke; there was nothing to say until they found what Cole had called Fossil, until they could decide if he'd had the right idea.

For the first time since they'd come to the Planet, John didn't feel like making any jokes. Cole had been a good guy, he'd done his best to make up for luring them into the test program, he'd done what they told him to do—and now he was gone, brutally savaged, dying in blood and pain on the floor of a cage.

Reston. Reston would pay for it, and if the best way to get to him was to unleash some Umbrella monster, so be it. A fitting justice.

Screw the code book. If Fossil's as badass as Cole seemed to think, we release it and let the workers go and get out. Let it tear this place apart. Let it have Reston...

The hall curved right, then straightened out, continuing west. When they turned the corner, they saw the door on the right—and somehow, John just knew that it was Cole's lab room. He felt it.

He was right, after a fashion. The metal door opened—after they'd used a nine-millimeter key—into a small laboratory with counters and computers, which then opened into a surgical theater, all gleaming steel and porcelain. The door set into the back wall of the operating room was the one Cole had meant for them to find—and when they saw the creature, John could see why he'd insisted on telling them about it, even with his last gasping breaths. If it was even half as vicious as it looked, the Planet was history.

"Christ," Leon said, and John couldn't think of anything to add to that. They moved slowly toward the giant cylinder that sat in the corner of the large room, past the steel autopsy table and trays of shining equipment, finally stopping in front of the tube. The lights in the room were off, but there was a directional light aimed at the container from the ceiling, illuminating the thing. The Fossil.

The tube was fifteen feet high and at least ten in diameter, filled with a clear red liquid—and enveloped in the fluid, attached to tubes and wires that ran through the top, was a monster. A nightmare.

John imagined that it was called Fossil because of what it looked like, at least partly—some kind of a dinosaur, though not one that had ever walked the Earth. The ten-foot-tall creature was some pale color, its pebbled flesh a glowing pink because of the red liquid that surrounded it. There was no tail, but it had the thick skin and powerful legs of a dino. It was obviously built to walk upright, and though it had the small eyes and heavy, rounded snout of a carnivorous dinosaur, a T. Rex or velociraptor, it also had long, thickly muscled arms and hands with slender, grasping fingers. As impossible as it was, it looked like the mutant offspring of a man and a dinosaur.

What were they thinking? Why—why make something like this?

It was asleep, or in some kind of coma, but it was definitely alive. Connected to a thin hose was a small, clear mask that covered its nostril slits, and a band of plastic was tied around its thick snout to hold the giant jaws closed. John couldn't see them, but he had no doubt that there were rows of pointed teeth in the creature's wide and curving mouth. Its beady eyes were covered by some inner eyelid, a thin layer of purpled skin, and they could actually see the slow rise of its thick chest, the gently bobbing motions of its massive body in the red goo.

There was a clipboard hanging on the wall next to the Fossil, above a small monitor screen where thin green lines blipped silently across in fading pulses. Leon picked the clipboard up, flipping through the pages as John just stared, awed and disgusted. One of its spidery hands twitched, the eight-inch fingers curling into a loose fist.

"Says here that it's slated for autopsy in three

and a half weeks," Leon said, scanning. "'Specimen will remain in stasis,' blah blah blah... 'when it will be injected with a lethal dose of Hyptheion prior to dissection.'"

John glanced back at the autopsy table, saw the folded steel leaves on either side and three bone saws tucked underneath. The table had apparently been built to accommodate larger animals.

"Why keep it alive at all?" John asked, turning back to the sleeping Fossil. It was hard not to look; the creature was compelling, horrid and marvelous, an aberration that demanded attention.

"Maybe so the organs will be fresh," Leon said, then took a deep breath. "So... do we do it?"

That's the million dollar question, isn't it? We won't have the codes—but Umbrella will have one less playground for their twisted science. And maybe one less administrator.

"Yeah," John said. "Yeah, I think we do."

* * *

The men listened to him in silence, their faces thoughtful as they absorbed the horror that had invaded the Planet. The invasion from above, his call for help, how the gunmen had knocked him out after killing Henry Cole in cold blood. They asked no questions, just sat and drank coffee—someone had made coffee—and watched him speak. No one offered him a cup.

"...and once I recovered, I came here," Reston said, and ran a shaking hand through his hair, wincing appropriately. He didn't have to fake the tremors. "I—they're still out there, somewhere, perhaps planting explosives, I don't know... but we can stop them if we work together."

He could see in their blank eyes that it wasn't working, he wasn't inspiring them to act. He wasn't the best with people, but he could read them well enough.

They're not buying, work the Henry angle...

Reston's shoulders slumped, a quiver creeping into his voice. "They just shot him," he said, staring down in stunned sorrow. "He was begging, *pleading* for them to let him live, and they—they shot him."

"Where's the body?"

Reston looked up, saw that Leo Yan had spoken, one of the 3Ks' two handlers. Yan had no expression at all, leaning against the edge of the table with his arms crossed.

"What?" Reston asked, looking confused but knowing exactly what Yan was talking about. *Think, dammit, should have thought of this already—*

"Henry," someone else said, and Reston saw it was Tom Something-or-other, from construction. His gruff voice was openly skeptical. "They shot him, they knocked you out—so he's still by the cell block, right?"

"I—I don't know," Reston said, feeling too hot, feeling dehydrated from so much brandy. Feeling as though he might not be able to recover from the unexpected question. "Yes, he must be, unless they moved him for some reason. I woke up confused, dizzy, I wanted to get to you immediately, to make sure none of you had been injured. I didn't see if he was still there..."

They stared at him, a sea of rough faces that were no longer so neutral. Reston saw disbelief and disrespect, anger—and in the eyes of one or two, he saw what might have been hatred.

Why, what have I done to inspire such contempt? I'm their manager, their employer, I pay their goddamn wages—

One of the mechanics stood up from the table and addressed the rest of them, ignoring Reston completely. It was Nick Frewer, the one who seemed the most popular among the men.

"Who says we get outta here?" Nick said. "Tommy, you got the keys for the truck?"

Tom nodded. "Sure, but not for the gate or the storage shed."

"I got those," said Ken Carson, the cook. He stood up, too, and then most were standing, stretching and yawning, draining their cups.

Nick nodded. "Good. Everyone go pack up, be at the elevator in five—"

"Wait!" Reston said, unable to believe what he was hearing, that they would walk away from their moral duty, from their *obligations*. That they could ignore him. "There are more on the surface, they'll kill you! You have to help me!"

Nick turned and looked at him, his gaze calm and

insufferably patronizing. "Mr. Reston, we don't have to do anything. I don't know what's really going on, but I believe you're a liar—and I may not speak for everyone, but I know *I'm* not getting paid enough to be your bodyguard."

He smiled suddenly, his blue eyes sparkling. "Besides which, they're not after *us.*"

Nick turned and walked away, and Reston briefly considered shooting him—but he only had six bullets and no doubts that the men would turn on him if he injured one of their working-class pack. He thought about telling them that their lives were over, that he wouldn't forget their treachery, but he didn't want to waste his breath. And he didn't have time.

Hide.

It was all there was to do.

Reston turned his back on the insubordinates and hurried out, his mind grasping for places to go, rejecting them as too obvious, too exposed—

—and then he had it. The bank of elevators, around the corner from the medical facilities. It was perfect. No one would think to look in an elevator car that didn't even work, he could pry one open and be safe inside. At least for a while, until he thought of something else he could do.

Sweating in spite of the cool gray stillness that was the main corridor, Reston turned right and started to run.

* * *

After what seemed like hours of going down through the dark, of the cold and uncomfortable huddle on the deafeningly loud servicing lift, they hit bottom.

Or top, depending on how you look at it, Claire thought absently, looking down through the open panel as David's flashlight played across the plush interior, as the roaring motor wound down to silence. They'd landed on top of an elevator car, empty except for a stepladder pushed to one side.

They stepped off of the metal square, Claire relieved to be back on a reasonably solid surface. Riding down through an open elevator shaft where one false move could send you crashing to your death wasn't her idea of a good time.

"Think anyone heard us?" Claire asked, and saw David's silhouette shrug.

"If they were within a thousand feet of this thing, yes," he said. "Wait, I'll get the stepstool..."

Claire turned on her flashlight as David sat, grabbing the edges of the open panel and lowering himself down. As he moved the small ladder into place, Rebecca turned her flashlight on, and Claire caught a glimpse of her face.

"Hey, you okay?" she asked, worried. Rebecca looked sick, too pale and with dark, purplish half circles beneath her eyes.

"Yeah. I've been better, but I'll survive," she said lightly.

Claire wasn't convinced, but before she could pursue it any further, David called up to them.

"Alright—let your feet hang down, I'll guide them to the steps and then lift you down."

Claire motioned for Rebecca to go first, deciding that if she couldn't function, she'd probably say something. As David helped Rebecca down, though, it occurred to Claire that *she* wouldn't say anything.

I'd want to help, and I wouldn't want to be left behind; I'd keep going if it killed me...

Claire pushed the thoughts aside, lowering herself down through the elevator's roof. Rebecca wasn't as stubborn as she was, and she was a medic. She was fine.

As soon as she was down, David nodded at Claire and the two of them pulled at the cold metal doors, Rebecca holding her semi aimed loosely at the widening gap. When they'd managed to push the heavy doors a couple of feet apart, David stepped out first, then motioned for them to follow.

Wow.

She wasn't sure what she expected, but the gray hall of subtly lit concrete wasn't it. It stretched right, ending in a door, and left, a sharp turn about twenty feet from the elevator that headed east. Claire wasn't sure about the directions, but she knew that the elevator that had trapped Leon and John was roughly southeast—assuming it had gone straight down, anyway.

It was quiet, perfectly still and quiet. David tilted his head to the left, indicating that they would head that way, and Claire and Rebecca both nodded.

Might as well start at the elevator, see if we can figure out which way they headed...

Claire glanced at Rebecca again, not wanting to stare but uneasy about her health; she really didn't look so good, and as Rebecca turned toward the hall's corner, Claire hung back a little. She caught David's gaze, nodding slightly toward the young medic, frowning.

He hesitated, then nodded in turn, and she saw that he wasn't blind to her condition. At least there was that—

—and Rebecca let out a sharp cry of surprise, already at the corner—

—as a man in a blue suit leapt forward and grabbed her, knocking her gun out of her hand, putting a revolver to the side of her head. He locked one arm around her throat, tight, and turned wild, sweaty eyes in their direction, his finger on the trigger, a trembling grin on his aging face.

"I'll kill her! I'll do it! Don't make me do it!"

Rebecca clutched at his arm and he squeezed even tighter, his hands shaking, his blue eyes darting back and forth between David and Claire. Rebecca's eyes closed a little, her fingers dropping away, and Claire realized that she was too weak, that she was on the verge of collapse as it was.

"You people aren't going to kill me, just stay away! Stay away or I'll kill her!"

The barrel of the revolver was pressed to her skull; if David or she made a move...

They watched helplessly as the madman started backing around them, dragging Rebecca with him toward the door at the end of the hall.

TWENTY

It was frighteningly easy to bring fossil out of stasis. In a matter of moments, Leon had gotten into the monitoring program and figured out how to drain the giant cylinder. According to the digital timer that popped up on the screen, it would only take about five minutes once he entered the command.

Man, anyone working here could have done it, at any time. For such a paranoid company, Umbrella sure takes chances...

"Hey, look at this," John said, and Leon turned from the small computer, glancing warily at the monster. Even after surviving the hell of Raccoon, after fighting zombies and mammoth spiders and even a giant alligator, it was probably the strangest thing he'd ever seen.

John was standing at the wall across the room, staring up at a laminated picture. As Leon got closer, he saw that it was a map of the Planet, each area neatly labeled. The testing facility had a fairly simple layout, basically a giant corridor that surrounded the four phases, most of the rooms and offices on offshoots from the main hall.

John tapped a small square at the east, just across from where the service, elevator was. "Says 'test control/monitor room,'" he said, "and it's on the way out."

"You think Reston's holed up there?" Leon asked.

John shrugged. "If he was watching us in the test program, that's where he would have been—what I'm interested in is if he happened to leave his little black book lying around."

"Wouldn't hurt to check," Leon said. "It'll take the tube about five minutes to drain, we'd have time—assuming the elevator's not a problem."

John turned around to look at Fossil, asleep in its gel womb. "You think it'll actually wake up?"

Leon nodded. The stats that had been listed in the simple monitoring program all seemed to match up, its heart rate and respiration indicating deep sleep; no reason it wouldn't wake up once the warm nutrient bath was drained.

And it'll probably wake up cold, pissed, and hungry...

"Yeah," he said. "And we want to be gone when it does."

John smiled a little, not his usual grin but a smile, anyway. "Then let's get gone," he said softly.

Leon walked back to the computer, bathed in pale red light from the stasis tube. Fossil floated peacefully, a sleeping giant. A monstrosity, created by monstrous people and living a useless life in a place built for death.

Take it all down, Leon thought, and hit the "Enter" key. The timer started its count; they had five minutes.

* * *

David thought it was probably Reston, although there was no way to be sure. It didn't matter; all he cared about was how to get Rebecca away from him, and as the crazed man in the blue suit backed to the door, David realized that there was nothing he could do.

Not yet.

"Just go away! Leave me alone!" the man—Reston—shouted, and then he was gone. Rebecca was gone, and the weak, listless way she'd looked at them before the door closed scared David badly.

"What do we do?"

He looked at Claire, saw the anxiety and fear on her face, and made himself take a deep breath, blowing it out slowly. They wouldn't be able to do anything if they panicked—

—and we could very well get her killed.

"Stay calm," he said, feeling anything but. "We don't know the floor plan, we can't circle around behind him... we'll have to follow."

"But he—"

"Yes, I know what he said," David interrupted. "There's no alternative at this point. We let them get a safe distance, then follow, look for an opening."

And hope that he's not as unstable as he looks.

"Claire—this is stealth work, we can't afford to make a sound. Perhaps it would be better if you stayed here..."

Claire shook her head, a look of determination in her gray eyes. "I can do it," she said, firmly and clearly. She had no doubts, and though untrained, she'd proven herself to be quick and steady.

David nodded and they walked to the door to wait, *two minutes unless we hear an exit, crack the door for sound—*

He forced himself to take another deep breath, cursing himself for letting Rebecca come with them. She was exhausted and injured, she wouldn't be able to fight if he decided to tighten his arm a bit more about her throat...

No. Hang on, Rebecca. We're coming, and we can wait all night for him to make a slip, to find our opportunity.

They waited, David praying that Reston wouldn't hurt her, swearing that he'd cut out the man's liver and feed it to him if he did.

* * *

They looked for the elevator, not sprinting through the endless gray hall, but not taking their time about it, either. The cafeteria was empty, and a half-minute check of the bunk rooms satisfied John that the workers had gone. There were clear signs that the guys had been in a hurry to grab their shit and get out.

Hope Reston's still here, though...

As they ran north down the main corridor, John decided that if Mr. Blue was still in the control room, he'd knock him out. A good solid punch to the temple would do it, and if he didn't wake up before Fossil started to roam, too bad.

They ran past the small offshoot that connected the control room to the main hall, both of them panting, both of them aware that they needed a working elevator a hell of a lot more than they needed to screw with Reston. As Leon had said, they didn't want to be around for the Planet's grand finale.

The open panel in the wall and the small light above the "In use" sign were enough to make John grin like a kid, the relief a cool and sweeping wave; they'd taken a big risk deciding to let Fossil out before securing their escape route.

Leon hit the recall button, looking just as relieved. "Two, two-and-a-half minutes," he said, and John nodded.

"Just a quick look," he said, and turned back toward the small passage across the hall. Leon was out of ammo, but John still had a few rounds in the M-16 in case Reston did anything stupid.

They hurried to the door at the end of the hall and found it unlocked. John went first, sweeping the large room with the rifle, then whistling in awe at the setup.

"Damn," he said softly. A line of black leather chairs

faced an entire wall of screens. Deep red plush carpet. A shining silver console, sleek and ultramodern, a table that looked like solid white marble behind it.

At least we don't have to dig through any clutter....

Except for a coffee mug and a silver flask on the console, there was nothing to see. No papers or office stuff, no personal items, no secret code books.

"Probably ought to get going," Leon said. "I'm estimating time here, I'd hate to be a couple minutes off."

"Yeah, okay. Let's—"

There was movement on one of the wall screens, midway through the second row from the top. John stepped closer to the monitor, wondering who the hell it could be, *the employees got out and that's two people, can't be—*

"Oh, shit," John said, and felt his stomach drop, a sickening plunge that seemed to go on and on, his horrified gaze fixed to the screen.

Reston, with a gun. Dragging Rebecca through some hall, his arm around her throat. Rebecca's feet half-dragging on the floor, her head hanging, her arms slack.

"Claire!"

John glanced away, saw Leon staring at a second monitor, saw David and Claire, armed, moving quickly down another featureless corridor.

"Can we refill the tube?" John barked, his gut still lurching, feeling more terrified by the sight of their friends than he had all night, *that miserable bastard's got 'becca—*

"I don't know," Leon said quickly, "we can try, but we've gotta go *now*—"

John stepped back from the wall, searching the pictures for one of the laboratory area, his exhaustion falling away as fresh adrenaline pounded into his system.

There, a dark room, a single light in the corner pointed at the tube, at the moving, thrashing thing inside. In seconds, dripping hands plunged through the clear matter, tearing, shattering, a massive, pallid, reptilian leg stepping through.

Too late: Fossil was out.

TWENTY-ONE

The creature designated Tyrant Series ReH1a, more commonly known as Fossil, was motivated purely by instinct and it only had one: eat. All of its actions stemmed from that single, primal urge. If there was something between it and food, Fossil destroyed it. If something attacked, tried to stop it from food, Fossil killed it. There was no reproductive impulse, because Fossil was the only member of its species.

Fossil woke hungry. It sensed food, picking up on electrical charges in the air, scents, distant heat—and destroyed the thing that held it. The environment was unfamiliar to Fossil, but not important; there was food, and it was hungry.

At ten feet tall and weighing roughly a thousand pounds, the wall that stood between Fossil and food didn't stop it for long. Past that was another wall, and then another—and the rich feels and smells of food were very close, so close that Fossil experienced the closest thing it had to an emotion: it *wanted,* a state of being that went beyond hunger, a powerful extension of its instinct that encouraged it to move faster. Fossil would eat almost anything, but living food always made it want.

The wall that stopped it from food was thicker and harder than the others, but not so much that it could stop Fossil. It ripped through the layers of substance and was in a strange place, nothing organic there but the moving, screeching food.

Food ran at it, hard to see but smelling quite strongly. Food raised a claw and swiped at Fossil, crying in fury, its desire to attack and kill; Fossil knew this because of the smell. Within seconds, Fossil was surrounded by food, and again, it wanted. The animals that were food howled and screamed, dancing and leaping, and Fossil reached out and picked up the closest.

Food had sharp talons, but Fossil's hide was thick. Fossil bit into the food, tearing a great chunk from the writhing body, and was fulfilled. Its sense of purpose was met so long as it chewed and swallowed, hot blood dripping down its throat, hot flesh ripping between its teeth.

The other food animals continued to attack, making it easy for Fossil to eat. Fossil ate all of the food animals in a short period of time, and its metabolism used the food almost as quickly, giving Fossil strength to find more food. It was an extremely simple process, one that continued as long as Fossil was awake.

Finished with the dark and cavernous room that had housed the screaming food, Fossil licked blood off its fingers and opened its senses, searching for its next meal. In seconds, it knew that there was more, living and moving close by.

Fossil wanted. Fossil was hungry.

TWENTY-TWO

The girl was sick, her skin clammy, her attempts to get away from him pathetic and weak. Reston wished he could get rid of her, just drop her and run, but he didn't dare. She was his ticket through the forces on the surface; surely they wouldn't kill one of their own.

Still, he wished the stupid girl wasn't so ill; she was slowing him down, hardly able to walk, and he had no choice but to continue dragging her along, north through the back corridor, then east at the far corner of the facility, heading for the connecting door to the cell block. From the cells the service elevator was a two-minute walk.

Almost there, almost done with this impossible, incredible night, not much farther...

He was an extremely important man, he was a respected member of a group that had more money and power than most countries, he was Jay Wallingford Reston—and here he was being hunted in his own facility, forced to take a *hostage,* to hold a gun to the head of a sick girl and sneak out like some criminal; it was ludicrous, just unbelievable.

"Too tight," the girl whispered, her voice strangled and rasping.

"Too bad," he answered, continuing to drag her along by her slender throat, her head tucked through his arm; she should have thought of that before she decided to invade the Planet.

He pulled her through the door that led into the cell block, feeling better with each step he took. Each was another step closer to escape, to survival. He would *not* be gunned down by some pious, self-righteous group of visionless thugs; he'd kill himself first.

Past the empty cells, almost to the door—and the girl stumbled, falling into him so hard that she almost knocked him down. She gripped him tightly, trying to regain her balance, and Reston felt a sudden insane rush of anger at her, of rage.

Stupid bitch, assassin, spy, I should shoot you right here, now, blow your slack, stupid brain across the walls—

He regained control before he could pull the trigger, but the loss of composure frightened him a little. It would have been a mistake, and a costly one.

"Do that again and I'll kill you," he said coldly, and kicked at the door that led into the main hall, pleased at the merciless quality of his voice. He sounded strong, like a man who wouldn't hesitate to kill if it served his purposes—which, he was coming to discover, was what he was.

Through the door and into the hall—

"Let her go, Reston!"

John and Red were at the corner, both of them with weapons trained on *him*. Blocking the path to the elevator.

Immediately, Reston dragged the girl back, they'd just have to go back into the cell block while he decided how to handle—

"Forget it," Red growled. "They're right behind you, we saw them tailing you. You're trapped."

Reston pushed the gun barrel against the girl's head, desperate, *I've got the hostage, they can't, they have to let me go—*

"I'll kill her!" He backed up again, moving toward the anteroom of the test program, the girl staggering to stay on her feet.

"And then we'll kill you," John said, not a whisper of lie in his deep voice. "If you hurt her, we'll hurt *you*. Let her go and we leave."

Reston reached the closed metal door and reached around for the control panel, hitting the button that would unlock the gate and the hatch into One.

"You can't possibly expect me to believe that," he sneered as the sheet metal slid up; there was only one Dac left alive and he'd left their kennel open—*I can climb, I can still get away from them, it's not too late!*

At that second, the door to the cell block opened and the other two stepped out—stepped in between the gunmen and him, and he acted before he had time to think, taking his chance.

Reston pushed the girl away, hard, throwing her toward all four of them and he jumped left in the same motion, hitting the hatch with his shoulder. The door into One flew open and he was through, slamming it closed. There was a bolt and he threw it, the metal making a sound like music.

As long as he stayed away from the clearings, he was safe. They couldn't touch him.

* * *

Strong hands caught her before she could crash into the ground—and she could *breathe* again—and John and Leon were alive... the relief was an ocean of warmth rising up over her, making her feel even weaker than she already was. The extended chokehold had taken most of what little strength she'd had. In fact, now that she thought about it, Rebecca felt an awful lot like death on two legs; like crap on a cracker as she used to say when she was a child...

Claire held her steady—it was Claire's strong hands that she'd felt—and everyone gathered around her, John picking her up easily. Rebecca closed her eyes, relaxing into her exhaustion.

"Are you alright?" David asked, and she nodded, relieved and happy that they were together again, that no one had been hurt—

—*no one but me, anyway*—

—and she knew that once she had a chance to rest, she'd be fine.

"We have to get out of here, *now*," Leon said, an urgency in his voice that made Rebecca open her eyes, the warm and sleepy feelings instantly gone.

"What is it?" David asked, his voice going just as sharp.

John turned and started carrying her down the hall, quickly, calling back over his shoulder. "We'll tell you on the way up, but we've gotta go ASAP, no joke."

"John?" she said, and he looked down at her, throwing her a small smile, his dark eyes telling a different story.

"We'll be fine," he said, "you just relax, start making up stories to tell us about your war wounds."

She'd never seen him look so uneasy, and she started to tell him that she was wounded, not stupid—

—when a tremendous, thundering crash came from somewhere ahead, a sound like walls being torn down, like glass exploding, like a bull in a china shop—

—and John spun around, running back the way they'd come—then she couldn't *see* but heard Claire's gasp, heard David say, "Oh, my God," in breathless disbelief, and felt her tired heart start to pound in fear.

Something very bad was coming.

TWENTY-THREE

Goddammit, not fast enough—

In a cloud of dust and rubble, cracked concrete and plaster, Fossil burst into the hall across from the elevator like a vision of hell. Its snout and hands were red, splashes of violent color against its sickly white skin, its giant, impossible body filling the corridor.

"Clip!" Leon screamed, not taking his gaze from the looming monster, still a hundred feet in front of them and not nearly far enough. He drew his empty H&K and ejected the clip, barely aware that it was Claire who handed him another as Fossil took a step toward them—

—and David was firing the M-16, the clatter of rounds blasting through the long hall, Fossil taking another huge step forward as Leon slapped the clip home. John was suddenly next to him, grabbing a rifle mag from David, Claire on David's other side, all of them targeting the creature.

Leon found the monster's right eye and squeezed the trigger, the roar of his nine-millimeter lost in the combined explosive firepower, all of them firing—

—*bambambam,* the sounds blending together, deafening, Fossil tilting its head to one side as if curious, taking another step into the wall of bullets.

"Fall back!" David shouted, and Leon backed up a step, horrified by Fossil's lack of wounds. If they were causing it any pain at all Leon couldn't see it, but it was all they had. He tried for the eye again—

—and heard Claire screaming something, glanced away long enough to see that she had a grenade out, that she was handing it to David.

"Go, go, go!" David shouted, and John grabbed Leon's arm and they turned and ran, Claire pacing them, Leon praying that they were far enough away not to be hit by the shreds of hot metal.

* * *

Claire ran, terrified, thinking that she'd never seen anything like it. A blood-painted fishbelly nightmare, a curved grin of wickedly sharp teeth and its *hands,* the too-long fingers stained red—

—*what is it,* how *is it*—

"Fire in the hole!" David screamed, and Claire pushed off the cement, trying to fly, seeing in that airborne second Rebecca's pale, strained face, the girl slumped against the back wall still a hundred feet away—

—and *BOOM,* she *was* flying, John to her right, a warm body falling against her back—and they all hit the floor, Claire trying to take it on the shoulder, landing too heavily on her arm instead.

Ow ow ow!

David had thrown himself against her, either on purpose or from the blast, and as she sat up, turning, she saw him grimace in pain. She saw two, three pieces of dark metal stuck to his back, pinning the black fleece to his skin, and reached out to help him—

—and saw the monster still standing. Brushing at its chest and belly, at the blackened patches from the frag grenade. A few shards had pierced its flesh, but she thought—it was hard to tell from its silence—from the way it took another step toward them it looked seemingly unfazed. It opened its mouth, its heavy lizard jaws—exposing strings of some unknown meat stuck between its jagged teeth. Silently, it took another step forward, grinning its carnivorous grin, and Claire imagined that she could smell the bloody meat of its breath, of whatever lay rotting in its guts—

SNAP OUT OF IT!

She crawled to her feet, ignoring the pain in her arm, reaching down to grab David's outstretched hand and pull him up. The second he was on his feet she pointed her nine-millimeter and started to fire again, knowing it wasn't enough, not knowing what else to do.

* * *

Four points of injury, all in his upper back, all burning and sharp. David hissed air between his teeth, decided the pain was bearable, and put it aside until further notice. The freakish monster wasn't down, it may have slowed but it wasn't stopping, and they didn't have anything bigger to throw at it than what they'd already tried.

Run, we'll have to run—

Even as he thought it, he was opening his mouth to shout, to be heard over John and Leon and Claire as they emptied their weapons, the rounds as useless as the grenade had been.

"John, get Rebecca! Fall back, we can't stop it!"

John was gone, Leon and Claire sidling backwards, firing just as he was—on the slim chance that it was doing some damage, that one of the rounds might hit something that could be hurt.

"David, we could go through the test, reinforced steel!" John shouted, and David wasn't sure what he was talking about but he understood "reinforced steel." It probably wouldn't stop the mutant animal, but it might slow it down enough for them to regroup, to work out some plan.

"Do it!" David shouted, and the monster took two, three strides toward them, apparently no longer interested in a hesitant approach. At that speed, it would be on them in scant seconds.

"*Run,* after John!" he screamed, and gave Leon and Claire a heartbeat of cover before he turned and ran after them.

Steel, reinforced steel—A mantra that looped through his racing thoughts as he sprinted, Claire and Leon turning the corner, the cement curve whipping past him as he saw Rebecca and John in the room at the end of the hall. The room where the madman had gone.

"David, hit the buttons, close the door!" John shouted, and David saw the controls, the small lights above the rounded knobs, and veered toward them, still at a dead run.

Claire and Leon were inside. David shot his arm out and slammed his open hand into the largest button on the panel, hoping he'd chosen the right one—

—and he was through, even as a sheet of metal guillotined the air behind him, close enough for him to feel it on the back of his neck.

He spun around just in time to see the heavy white body of the hybrid creature slam into the door, its chest smashing against the thick, warped window set into the thick metal. The door shivered in its tracks, and David could see that it wouldn't stand for long.

Please hold, just for a moment—

He turned, saw Leon at the smaller hatch on the south wall, saw the horror in his eyes, the color leached from his face, his trembling hand on the door's lever.

"Locked," he said, and outside, the monster smashed into the door again.

* * *

Reston heard the noise when he was trying to figure out how to climb into the Av kennel. The pen was about twelve feet off the ground, an open hole in the wall, and there was no ladder; the closest tree was a good seven feet away, impossible—but his only other way out of the test was the way he'd come, and he didn't dare go back out into the main hall. He'd about made up his mind to attempt climbing the tree to try the jump when the rending crashes had seeped into the room from Phase Two.

Reston walked toward the connecting door, curious in spite of his fear. The phases were heavily soundproofed; a noise like that could only be from a bomb, or a wrecking crew...

...which means bomb. They've planted explosives after all, the monsters.

Reston waited by the door for a moment, but didn't hear anything else. The lone Dac let out a cry from somewhere across the chamber, the fight apparently taken out of it with the loss of its siblings; it hadn't tried to attack.

Explosives....

Phase Two was directly behind control, a double-thick wall between them, which had to mean that the renegades had blown up the control center, the most important—and most expensive—room in the Planet. They couldn't have chosen a better target; the facility was practically worthless with control destroyed.

But perhaps they've given me another way out... Reston wasn't going to make any bets as to whether or not the barbarous mercenaries had finally gone, leaving the broken remains of the Planet behind—

—*but if they have...*

If they had, he'd be able to walk out. Maybe just walk away—and not just from the Planet, but from White Umbrella. He was reasonably certain that Jackson would kill him for what had happened... but not if Reston disappeared.

A few hundred thousand to Hawkinson, a ride to a safe place....

It could work, if he timed it right, if he changed his name and identity and went far, far away. It *would* work.

Nodding to himself, he cracked open the door to Two, not sure what to expect—but it was still a surprise to see the massive, gaping holes in two of the desert's walls and the cement and wood and steel blown to pieces; each ragged opening was at least ten feet across, perhaps twenty feet high. He didn't see smoke anywhere, but imagined that the saboteurs had used some high-tech compound, some material that scum like that always seemed to have access to.

The heat was still high, and the lights were blazing, but it was definitely cooler with the new ventilation— and though he stood for long seconds listening, he didn't hear a sound that might indicate their presence. Unless it was some kind of trap...

Reston shook his head, amused by his own paranoia. Now that he'd decided to be free, to leave behind the ruins of his life, he felt a kind of elation. A sense of new possibilities, even of rebirth. They were gone, their mission accomplished, the Planet wasted.

Reston walked across the hot sands, stepping over the pieces of Scorp scattered about, finally climbing the shifting dune to peer into the hole.

My God, they managed to get everything, didn't they?

The destruction was nearly total, the gaping hole almost exactly where the monitor wall had been. Thick shards of glass, bits of wire and circuitry, a faint scent of ozone—that was all that was left of the brilliantly designed video-retrieval system. Four of the leather chairs had been knocked off their welded mounts, the one-of-a-kind marble table had actually cracked in two—and in the northeast corner of the room there was another giant, ragged hole surrounded by debris.

And through that hole....

Reston could actually *see* the elevator. The working, running elevator, the lights engaged, the platform recalled.

Was it a trap? It seemed too good to be true—but then he heard a distant pounding, somewhere off by the cell block, and thought that luck was finally with him; the employees had left, the sound could only be the blasted ex-S.T.A.R.S. team. Far enough away that he'd be halfway to the surface before they could make it back.

Reston grinned, amazed that it would end like this; it seemed so anticlimactic somehow, so mundane...

...and am I complaining? No, no complaints. Not from me.

Reston stepped through the hole, moving carefully to avoid the sharp glass.

* * *

The battle with the food animals had made it hungry, had made it crave; that there was a strong wall in Fossil's way made it only more eager to eat, to fulfill its purpose. It pounded at the strong obstacle, feeling the matter shift, becoming less rigid—

—and although it wouldn't take much more to get at the animals, Fossil suddenly smelled new food. Back the way it had come, food, open and exposed, nothing between it and Fossil.

It would come back after it had eaten. Fossil turned away and ran, hungry and wanting, determined to eat before the food could move away.

* * *

As soon as Fossil turned and ran, John started to kick at the steel door, realizing that it was their only chance. The incredible beating that the monster had given it made it easy, the thick metal half off its tracks already.

Claire and Leon started kicking. In seconds, they'd knocked it far enough from the metal indentation that it fell off, clattering to the floor—and seconds after that, they were running, running for the elevator, David carrying Rebecca and all of them silent. Fossil would be back, they all knew it, and they didn't stand a chance against it.

"NO! NO! NO!"

A man, screaming, and as John rounded the corner, he saw that it was Reston, saw him sprinting down the long corridor, Fossil closing fast.

They ran, John wondering how long it would take the monster to eat an entire human. And as they reached the elevator, leapt through the doors, Leon pulling the gate down—

—they all heard the wailing scream rise to an inhuman pitch—and then cut off sharply, stopped by a heavy wet *crunch*.

The elevator started to rise.

TWENTY-FOUR

Rebecca was falling asleep, the lull of the elevator as soothing as the sound of David's heartbeat. As tired as she was, she lifted one incredibly heavy hand to the flat black book tucked into the waistband of her pants. Reston hadn't even noticed, apparently hadn't suspected that she could fake a fall with the best of them.

She thought about telling the others, breaking the tired silence in the rising elevator to give them the news, then decided it could wait; they deserved a pleasant surprise.

Rebecca closed her eyes, resting. They still had a long way to go, but the tide was turning; Umbrella would pay for its crimes. They would see to it.

EPILOGUE

With David and John supporting young Rebecca, and Leon and Claire smiling at one another like lovers, the five weary soldiers trudged off the screen and out into the gently blossoming Utah morning.

Sighing, Trent leaned back in his chair, idly twisting his onyx ring. He hoped they'd take a day or two to rest before heading to their next great battle... perhaps the last great battle; they deserved a bit of rest after all they'd suffered. Really, if any one of them survived what was surely ahead, he'd have to see that they were amply rewarded.

Assuming I'm still in a position to bequeath gifts...

He would be, of course. If and when Jackson and the others finally figured out what part he was playing, he'd have to disappear—but there were half a dozen completely untraceable identities for him to choose from seeded around the world, each of them extremely wealthy. And White Umbrella didn't have the resources to track him down. They had money and power, true, but they simply weren't smart enough.

I've managed to get this far, haven't I?

Trent sighed again, reminding himself not to gloat, at least not yet. It wouldn't pay to be overconfident, he knew; better men than he had died at the hands of Umbrella. In any case, either he'd be dead or they would. End of problem, one way or the other.

He stood up, stretching his arms over his head and shrugging the tension from his shoulders; the satellite "pirate" had allowed him to see and hear almost all of it, and it had been a long and eventful night. A few hours sleep, that was what he needed. He'd arranged to be out of touch until about noon, but then he'd have to put a call in to Sidney—and the old tea-drinker would be nearly frantic by then, along with the rest of them. The mysterious Mr. Trent's services would be desperately sought after, and he'd have to catch the next plane out; as much as he wanted to watch Hawkinson return and fumble through putting Fossil down, he needed the sleep more.

Trent turned off the screens and walked from his operations room—a living room with a few rather expensive adjustments—into the kitchen, which was just a kitchen. The small house in upstate New York was his sanctuary if not his home; it was from here that he conducted most of his work. Not the grandiose scheming he did on White Umbrella's behalf, but his *real* work. Were anyone to check, they'd find the three-room Victorian to be owned by a little old lady named

Mrs. Helen Black. A private joke, one all his own.

Trent opened the refrigerator and took out a bottle of mineral water, thinking of how Reston had looked in his last moment, staring into the face of his own demise. Lovely work, that, using Fossil against him; it was really too bad about Cole. The man could have been an asset to the small but growing resistance.

Carrying the water upstairs, Trent used the bathroom and then walked down a short hall, wondering how much longer he had. In the first few weeks of his contact with White Umbrella, he'd half-expected to be called into Jackson's office and summarily shot at any given moment. But the weeks had stretched into months, and he hadn't caught even a whisper of doubt—from any of them.

In the bedroom, he laid out his clothes for the flight and then undressed, deciding that he would pack while he had his coffee, after calling Sidney. Turning off the light, Trent slipped into bed and sat for a moment, sipping at his bottled water, going over his meticulous plans for the next few weeks. He was tired, but his life's goal was finally within reach; it wasn't so easy to fall asleep when one was about to realize the culmination of three decades of planning and dreaming, of a wish so long-held that it had become who he was...

The final strokes, though. There were still several things that had to happen before he could finish, and most of those had to do with how well his rebels fared. He had faith in them, but there was always a chance that they might fail—in which case, he'd have to start over again. Not from scratch, but it would be a serious setback.

Eventually, though...

Trent smiled, setting his water on the nightstand and sliding beneath the thick down comforter. Eventually, the evil of White Umbrella would be exposed to the light of day. Killing the players would be easier, but he wouldn't be satisfied with their deaths; he wanted to see them *destroyed,* financially and emotionally, their lives taken from them in every practical sense. And when that day came, when the leaders had finished watching their precious handiwork crumble to ash, he would be there. He'd be there to dance in the cemetery of *their* dreams, and it would be a fine day indeed.

As he so often did, Trent went over the speech in his mind, the speech that he'd spent a lifetime practicing for that day. Jackson and Sidney would have to be there, as well as the European "boys" and the financiers from Japan, Mikami and Kamiya. They all knew the truth, they had been coconspirators in the treachery...

I stand in front of them, smiling, and I say, "A little background, in case any of you have forgotten.

"Early in Umbrella's history—before there was such a thing as White Umbrella—there was a scientist working in their research and development sector named James Darius. Dr. Darius was an ethical and committed microbiologist, who, along with his lovely

wife, Helen—a doctor of pharmacology, in fact—spent untold hours developing a tissue-repair synthesis for their employers, one that James had created himself. This synthesis that took up so much of the Dariuses'' time was a brilliantly designed viral complex that— if properly developed—had the potential to greatly reduce human suffering, even one day to wipe out death by traumatic injury.

"Both James and Helen had the highest of hopes for their work—and they were so responsible, so loyal and trusting, that they went to Umbrella immediately, once they realized the potential of what they were designing. And Umbrella, Inc. also realized the potential. Except what they saw was a financial nosedive if such a miracle were to be released. Imagine all the money that a pharmaceutical company would lose if millions of people stopped dying each year; but then, imagine what money could be made if this viral complex could be designed to fit a military application. Imagine the power.

"With incentives like that, Umbrella really had no choice. They took the synthesis from Darius, they took the notes and research, and they turned it all over to a brilliant young scientist by the name of William Birkin, barely out of his teens and already the head of his own lab. Birkin was one of them, you see. A man with the same vision, the same lack of morals, a man they could use. And with their own puppet in place, they realized that having the good Doctors Darius around could prove to be inconvenient.

"So, there was a fire. An accident, it was said, a terrible tragedy—two scientists and three loyal assistants all burned up. Too bad, so sad, case closed—and so began the division of Umbrella known as White Umbrella. Bioweapons research. A playground for the filthy rich and their toadies, for men who'd lost anything resembling a conscience a long, long time ago." I smile again. "For men like you.

"White Umbrella had thought of everything, or so they believed. What they hadn't considered—either because they were too shortsighted or ignorantly dismissive—was the young son of James and Helen, their only child, away at boarding school when his parents were burned alive. Perhaps they simply forgot about him. But Victor Darius didn't forget. In fact, Victor grew up thinking about what Umbrella had done, dare I say obsessing over it. There came a time when Victor could think of nothing else, and that was when he decided to do something about it.

"To avenge his mother and father, Victor Darius knew he would have to be extremely clever and very, very careful. So he spent years just planning. And more years learning what he needed to know, and even more making the right contacts, moving in the right circles, being as devious and underhanded as his foe. And one day, he murdered Umbrella, just as they murdered his parents. It wasn't easy, but he was determined, and he'd devoted his entire life to the project."

I grin. I say, "Oh, and did I mention that Victor Darius changed his name? It was a bit of a risk, but *he decided to go with his father's middle name, or at least part of it. James Trenton Darius wasn't using it anymore, after all."*

The speech always changed a little, but the essentials stayed the same. Trent knew that he would never have the opportunity to deliver it to all of them at once, but it was the *idea* that had kept him going, all these many years. On nights when he'd been so enraged that he couldn't sleep, the retelling of the story had come to be a kind of bitter lullaby; he imagined the looks on their tired old faces, the horror in their faded eyes, their trembling indignation at his betrayal. Somehow, the vision always soothed his fury and gave him some small peace.

Soon. After Europe, my friends...

The thought followed him down into the dark, to the sweet, dreamless sleep of the righteous.

ABOUT THE AUTHOR

S.D. Perry is the author of several tie-in novels to popular series such as *Aliens*, *Alien vs. Predator*, *Star Trek* and *Star Trek: Deep Space Nine*. Perry also wrote the movie novelizations for *Timecop* and *Virus*. She is the daughter of bestselling sci-fi author Steve Perry and lives in Portland, Oregon with her husband and two children.

RESIDENT EVIL RETRIBUTION

THE OFFICIAL MOVIE NOVELIZATION

SCREENPLAY BY
PAUL W.S. ANDERSON
NOVELIZATION BY JOHN SHIRLEY

Just as she finds a safe haven, free from the Undead,
Alice is kidnapped by her former employers—the
Umbrella Corporation. Regaining consciousness,
she finds herself trapped in the most terrifying
scenario imaginable.

The T-virus continues to ravage the Earth,
transforming the world's population into legions
of flesh-eating monsters. Reunited with friends
and foes alike—Rain Ocampo, Carlos Oliveira, Jill
Valentine, Ada Wong, Leon S. Kennedy, and even
Albert Wesker—she must fight her way back to reality
in order to survive.

The countdown has begun, and the fate of the
human race rests on her shoulders.

For more fantastic fiction from Titan Books in the areas of sci-fi, fantasy, steampunk, alternate history, mystery and crime, as well as tie-ins to hit movies, TV shows and videogames:

VISIT OUR WEBSITE
TITANBOOKS.COM

FOLLOW US ON TWITTER
@TITANBOOKS